STARBUCKS NATION

STARBUCKS NATION

A NOVEL

CHRIS VER WIEL

ARCADE PUBLISHING ★ NEW YORK

FIRST EDITION

This is a work of fiction. Names, characters, places, and incidents are either the work of the author's imagination or are used fictitiously.

Title page photograph by Floyd Anderson / iStockphoto

Library of Congress Cataloging-in-Publication Data

Ver Wiel, Chris.
Starbucks nation : a novel / Chris Ver Wiel. —1st ed.
p. cm.
ISBN 978-1-55970-868-5 (alk. paper)
1. Screenwriters—Fiction. 2. California, Southern—Social life and customs—Fiction. I. Title.

PS3622.E44S73 2008
813'.6—dc22 2007039963

Published in the United States by Arcade Publishing, Inc., New York
Distributed by Hachette Book Group USA

Visit our Web site at www.arcadepub.com
Visit the author's Web site at www.StarbucksNationNovel.com

10 9 8 7 6 5 4 3 2 1

Designed by James Jayo

EB

PRINTED IN THE UNITED STATES OF AMERICA

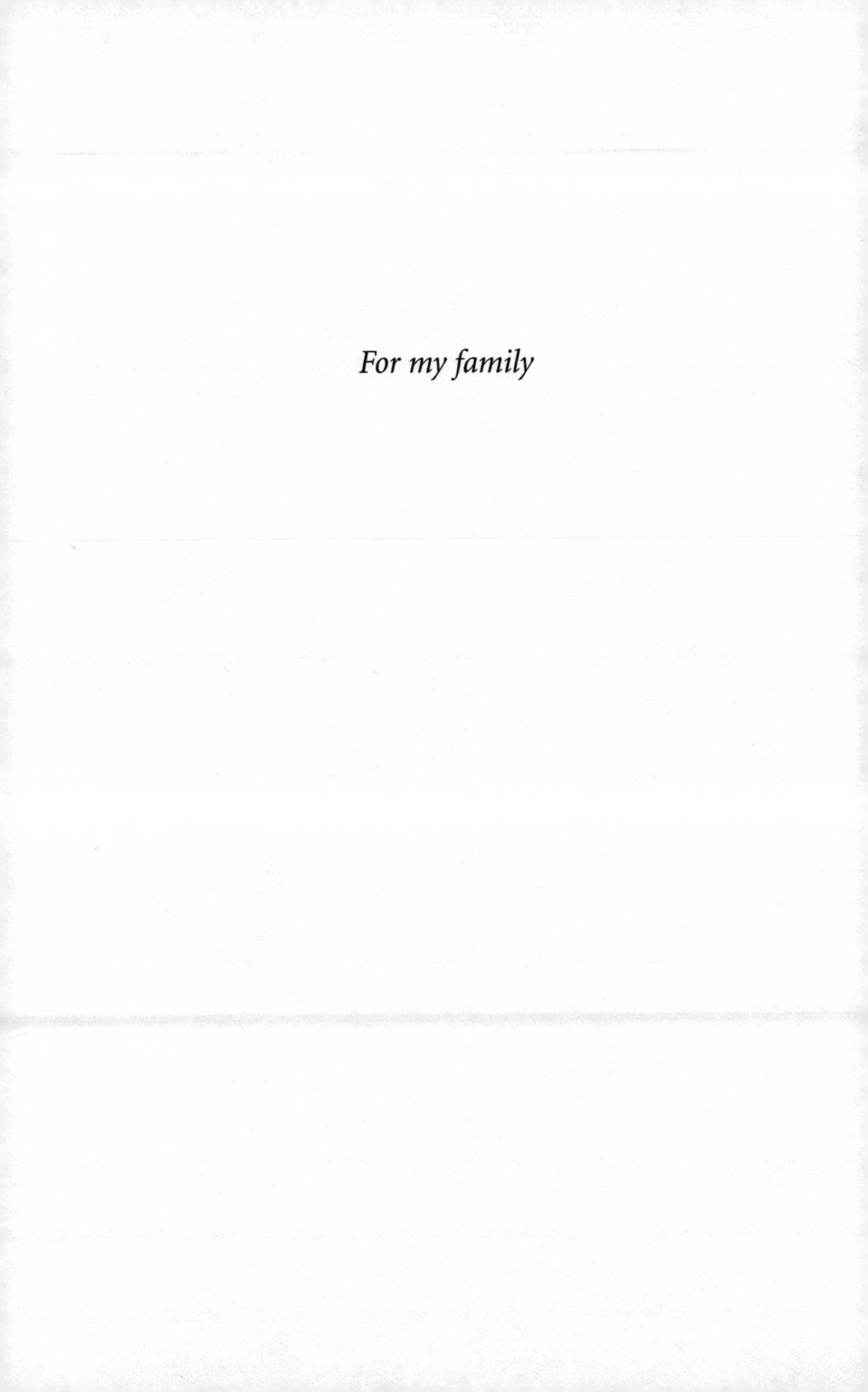

For my family

It is not the critic who counts: not the man who points out how the strong man stumbles or where the doer of deeds could have done better. The credit belongs to the man who is actually in the arena, whose face is marred by dust and sweat and blood, who strives valiantly, who errs and comes up short again and again, because there is no effort without error or shortcoming, but who knows the great enthusiasms, the great devotions, who spends himself for a worthy cause; who, at the best, knows, in the end, the triumph of high achievement, and who, at the worst, if he fails, at least he fails while daring greatly, so that his place shall never be with those cold and timid souls who knew neither victory nor defeat.

—Theodore Roosevelt

STARBUCKS NATION

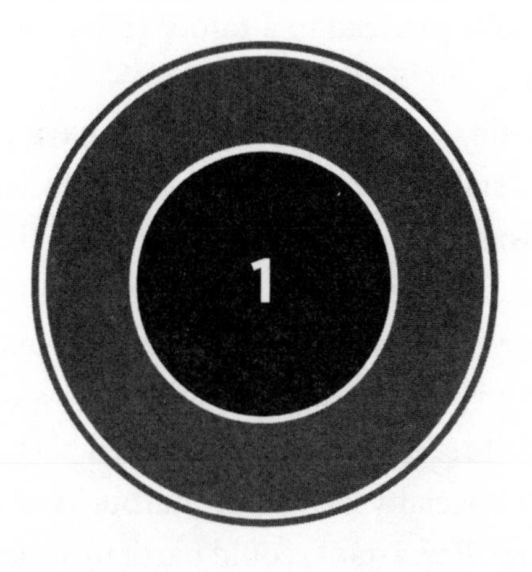

THE SECRET HANDSHAKE

It was the dishwasher at the hotel bar who taught me the secret handshake. He looked like he'd know — a guy with that kind of meth addiction knows how to get a good night's sleep.

The secret handshake consists of two tablets of over-the-counter pain medication with "P.M." on the box, two tabs of over-the-counter allergy medication with no initials on the box, one capful of that late-night, sniffling and sneezing, so-you-can-rest medicine — all downed with one large glass of red wine or alcoholic beverage of your choice. The handshake should be administered no more than one half hour before your scheduled time of departure.

As for your glass of red wine or alcoholic beverage, I

suggest you not enjoy it leisurely. The inconsistent timetable of the handshake can lead to a rather embarrassing spill that may be mistaken for a weak bladder or — worse yet, as in my case — red stains on white T-shirts that have prompted the hotel laundry staff to identify me mistakenly as Italian.

The dishwasher credited with the handshake is thin, pale, tattooed — and forgettable. I have seen him forty days in a row. His name is Jerry, or Barry, or Larry — maybe that's it. Yeah, Larry. Larry Forgettable tells the same stories over and over again. He breeds pit bulls. He named his last batch after the sizes and specialty drinks at Starbucks, the only other place that Larry Forgettable could participate as a member of the world's work force. This of course is due to the extensive spider-web tattoo that climbs up his neck to frame a very weak chin.

I learned the handshake thirty-eight days ago, my third night in forty at a swanky Sunset Strip hotel. Eleven P.M., three light beers, five glasses red wine, three shots tequila, and one of those licorice drinks served with a coffee bean. Appropriate since they usually give coffee to people who drink too much.

Day three was the third time Larry Forgettable had relived his fury that Venti had turned out to be the runt of the litter. This was a distinction he was sure would befall Pumpkin Latte. And then the inevitable puppy update. Venti had developed a limp. Tall and Grande had found suitable homes with insecure men with the all-popular moustache-and-tattoo combination. Scrappy-cino was returned for biting the youngest child of the senior member of the hotel security staff. Fingers crossed for Dopio; he hadn't bitten any children yet. Pumpkin Latte slept in the laundry room of a West Hollywood lesbian couple who met in Target's management program. They were trying to have a baby, although I was assured that this was not why they got Pumpkin Latte.

A sudden shift in Larry's forgettable eyes interrupted his joyful speechification. He looked across the bar at me. Then he looked away ever so slightly, as if he'd just remembered where he'd hidden his bong. After that, he couldn't make eye contact. I knew exactly what that meant. He recognized me. I know people recognize me when they can't make eye contact. When they do, they talk too fast. *You were in that movie, right? That movie with the guy who fucks his mom's mink glove? You're the guy who throws the glove through his girlfriend's windshield!*

I have written nine movies and directed four of them. I have won three Independent Spirit awards; was selected for Director's Fortnight at the Cannes Film Festival; won the Audience Award at the Sundance Film Festival — not once but *twice;* and have even been nominated for an Academy Award for screenwriting. All anyone remembers is the angry teenager who defiled his mother's handwear. Nobody cares about all the dead people on the train who find redemption, the con man who finally goes straight, or the millionaire base jumper who adopts a ten-year-old boy — just some horny little bastard who discovers that safe sex really does mean wearing a glove.

It was the first screenplay I had ever written, a teen comedy with heart. Why not? I was young, immature, and in dire need of love and attention. The infamous scene in question was shot on the third day of a very short shoot. A paltry twenty-six-day schedule with a two-and-a-half-million-dollar budget. The actor originally cast in the role turned out to be a disaster. On top of his inability to deliver a line, the poor bastard actually threw, for lack of a better term, like a girl. After fifty-four takes — one of which included his knocking over a coffee urn and causing second-degree burns on the nether regions of a visiting executive — he was summarily dismissed. The director suggested that I step in and play the role. The role had been offered to me originally, but I declined. I gave no reason. Fact was, I was scared to death. The director never forced the issue. He knew the truth; we did write the screenplay together. But now necessity divined that I step in. Was this providence? Was this a platform for my secret ambition? Maybe this would make me famous. People would love me.

Take fifty-five, my first take. They rolled sound and camera. The director, my writing partner, my great friend, smiled paternally and called, "Action!" He nodded to assure me that I was in safe hands. I took a small breath, delivered my lines, and fired the weighted glove. *Bull's-eye.* It crashed right through the glass, the thumb poking inside and pointing miraculously at a picture of the happy couple hanging from the rearview mirror. Then the creative gods blessed us with one of those moments you could never dream up on your own. The weight in the thumb shifted, causing the digit to deflate like a limp penis. The set roared. Turns out a thumbs down isn't such a bad thing.

That was fifteen years ago. I was twenty-nine-years old, and this single event represented the first time anything good had ever happened to me. The scene became iconic. It was acted out and parodied everywhere. Late-night television, prime-time television, the morning shows. It was on the radio and T-shirts. Politicians alluded to the image when describing their opponents. It even made the front page of *Time* magazine. Iconic became mythic. A simple shift in weight became the seminal image for a whole generation.

It was the only time I ever stepped in front of a camera. If you ask me what I am, I'll tell you I'm a writer. Not an actor. Not a director. A writer.

Larry Forgettable rested his spider-web chin on his heavily tattooed hands. "How'd you get the thumb to do that? Was it electronic? Like some sort of robot glove?" Larry Forgettable was genuinely interested.

The bartender moved swiftly to admonish the future sleep guru. Seemed my Sunset Strip hotel had a policy against employees making personal contact with clientele. Where was the bartender when I was suffering through *Memoirs of a Pit Bull*? Probably took me for some indigent sociopath who enjoyed hearing that Pumpkin Latte had balls the size of a small cat. Forgettable Larry turned back to his glasses. I made a mental note to quit washing my hair with bar soap so as to avoid any future doubt that my presence in the hotel bar was justified.

The handshake changed my life forever. That all-powerful god known as my wireless provider heralded the event. My agent had been dodging calls from the studio for the better part of a month. He wanted to know if I was still suffering from writer's block and if I was any closer to delivering a draft for the studio to read. Which brings me to why I found myself drunk in the swanky Sunset Strip hotel bar on only the third day of forty. The darkness of big-time Hollywood had commissioned me to adapt a beautifully executed little novel: *The Chihuahua in the Blue Prada Bag.*

The original story takes place at a house in the Hamptons. A weekend with the rich and famous turns upside down when a man realizes the only one he can truly communicate with is his wife's Chihuahua. *The Chihuahua in the Blue Prada Bag* spent forty-five weeks atop the *New York Times* best-seller list. The book satirizes American pop culture, ridiculing everything from new technology to unbridled consumption. The theme that "reality" television will destroy art as we know it is sublime. The end of the book is the writer's personal coup d'etat, his own thumb in the windshield, so to speak. The Chihuahua persuades the husband to drive his wife's Porsche through a party and into the pool, a burning American flag in tow. The entire party converges on the sinking car. As the husband swims to safety, everyone finally hears the Chihuahua's voice: "The empire is dead! Long live China!"

Stunned faces stare at the Chihuahua. He responds to the dropped jaws: "That's right. *Dead!* All because of you fat, jobbed, tattooed fuckholes."

Of course we're not allowed to say that. This is Hollywood, for God's sake. No, we want an uplifting piece.

Let's set it in Malibu.

Let's have the dog solve the marriage issues of the husband and wife.

Let's give him some funny lines.

Everyone loves animal humor. Hey, could the Chihuahua find love, too?

Wait. Could the Chihuahua be a golden retriever? Like Old Yeller?

I'll see what I can do, you fat, jobbed, tattooed fuckholes.

The Chihuahua in the Blue Prada Bag won all kinds of awards. When I was first asked if I'd be interested in doing the adaptation, I declined. Why wreck something so perfect? Why destroy a comment on American culture so flawlessly executed?

The answer hit the front page of one of those contemptible magazines you find on every newsstand and at the front of every supermarket checkout line. There he was on the cover of *Us Weekly:* the writer, winner of a National Book Award. I had met him over dinner when the studio was first discussing the possibilities. I liked him. But the writer I met was no more. The man I met was shy and reserved. He didn't dare take credit for his success lest the creative gods take away his voice. He doted on his mousey wife and awkward children. I really did like him.

But that man died. Ironically, he became a blip on the radar himself. There he was on the front page: a new haircut, twenty pounds lighter. He put Prada in the title, so that's all he wore now. Oh, look at that, he started dating a popular reality star. What happened to his family? What? He took a break from writing? Of course he did. He lost his voice.

Fuck it. If he didn't care, why should I? I took the job. I lost my soul years ago. I know it all sounds so very Faustian. Welcome to moving pictures. It happens to everyone. All you need is an original thought. Insert a taste of fame, and the procedure begins. The procedure is when an original thought finds an unoriginal thinker who then exploits the thought and its creator ad nauseam. The procedure concludes when the most unoriginal of the thinkers, Hollywood, comes knocking.

Then a second procedure begins. It starts with the option agreement. An option agreement is a procedure whereby a producer — a fancy Hollywood term for "chimp in a suit" — firmly lodges his fist in the rectal cavity of the original thinker. The fist usually contains a wad of cash, so the original thinker doesn't forget who's in charge. Now that the chimp in a suit has firm control of the original thought, he and his team systematically strip away any and all soul that may actually cause the unoriginal thinkers of the world to think. Team Chimp digs a shallow pool, allowing the original thinker to drown in his own regret. Then they load the dead body into a Porsche and take it to a party.

One of the chimps responsible for the destruction of this original thought was Brad Berman. Chimp Brad Berman became famous in Hollywood for cutting hair. He has two salons, one in Beverly Hills and one in West Hollywood. He serves white wine with your cut. Only white wine. It's all Chimp Brad drinks. My writing partner used to say, "You should never trust a man who drinks white wine. He's either a fag or about to tell you he's a fag."

Brad the fag had a reality TV show for a while where he continually espoused his love for women. He met his current lover over a glass of white wine. Chimp Brad is one of my wife's best friends. That's how I got this job. My wife and Chimp Brad bought the film rights to the novel. My wife is famous in Hollywood — not for any particular talent, more for genealogy. Her father was "the cute one" in a boy band in the late sixties. Her mother is an heiress to a candy empire. My wife and white-wine-swilling Brad the Chimp bought the film rights to the book so both could realize their dream of becoming serious participants in the big screen world. My wife is an actress. She goes to a lot of Hollywood parties. Hollywood parties today are the acting schools of the fifties. Today's Actor's Studio is the *Vanity Fair* party after the Academy Awards.

My agent finally got around to the topic at hand. There would be no hedging on my part. "I don't have a draft yet." That I would confide. What I wouldn't share was that I didn't even have page one. I was four months in, and I hadn't written a word.

"Wouldn't you be more comfortable writing at home?" he asked.

"Of course I would. My wife is remodeling the fucking house." On Monday they started digging the pool. On Monday I checked in to this hotel.

"Yeah, I saw her on Letterman," he said. "How long is she going to be in New York?"

"The press junket is supposed to last three more weeks, I

think." My wife was promoting her new project, a slasher film called *A Killer in the Corn III*. On the poster, she's running through a cornfield at night. It sucked. "I'm having a hell of a time sleeping," I added. I've always had trouble sleeping.

"I'll try to steal some of my wife's sleeping pills for you," he said. Most agents lie, cheat, and steal and then put you to sleep with excuses. This one was offering to commit petty thievery in order to sedate me outright. Now that's what I call a working relationship. "I'll check in with you tomorrow," he said.

I motioned for the bartender and ordered my Sambuca with coffee bean. That was when Forgettable Larry thankfully thumbed his nose at hotel policy.

"You're having trouble sleeping?"

Thirty-eight blissful nights ago, I learned the secret handshake.

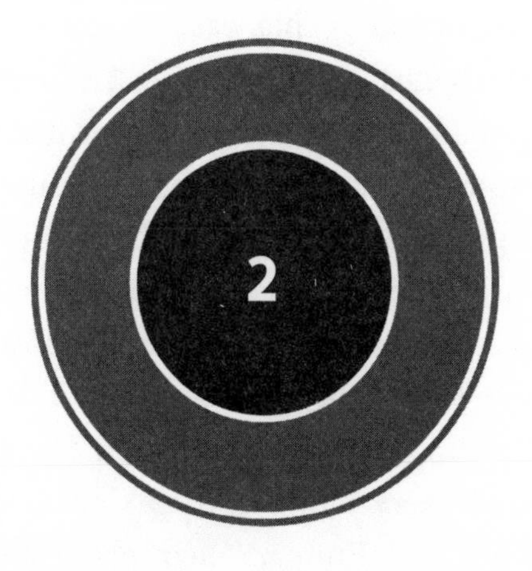

FORTY DAYS IN THE DESERT

Night forty in the swanky Sunset Strip hotel bar, 1:22 A.M. The handshake will be administered in thirty-eight minutes. I've already had one bottle of wine and am almost through another. Red is a great comfort in these trying times. I spent the better part of the evening being interviewed by a soft, doughy member of the crackerjack staff of *People* magazine.

My wife's publicist set up the interview in the hope that it would teach me how to swim in the shallow end of the gene pool. The boy was innocuous enough, no more than twenty-five years old, a member of that generation that has unbelievable self-esteem. Why not? Their parents filled their little heads with the idea that they could be whatever they wanted to be. That their wants and needs were more important than society's. Self before duty. That was why Emile Samarjian answered his cell phone five times during the interview. Emile's parents admired Zola. It was a no-brainer that young Emile would grow up to be a senior staff writer at the hard-hitting journalistic juggernaut that is *People* magazine.

Why does everyone in his generation have such well-thought-out names? Movie-star names like Brandon, Ethan, Jake, and Jason. Josh, Liam, Nicholas, and Tyler. Traditional names like Christopher become Topher. The girls can't escape, either. For every Jennifer, there's an Ashley, Brittany, Caitlyn, Dakota, and Emma. Their play dates were with Hannah, Madison, Olivia, Samantha, and Sarah. Whenever they went outside, they wore helmets. They all grew up with cable, computers, SpellCheck, and cellular options. Instant gratification is their mantra.

Who the hell was he talking to? Why didn't he at least get up from the table? Why should he? There was nowhere to go. Everywhere you looked, somebody was talking on a cell phone. It was quiet at my table. How did he get so fat? Why is everyone in his generation so fat? Maybe self-esteem, self-confidence, and inner journeys are high in carbs. Could following your bliss and manifesting your future have trans fats? Was Emile's true inner self filled with creamy nougat?

His laugh was like a swagger. I hated it. Emile was supremely confident. His parents chose to bring this joyous angel into the world. They were card-carrying members of the peace-and-love generation who laid down their protest signs for jobs in real estate and an eco-friendly law firm. Half a percent of every malpractice and libel settlement Emile's father won helped save the rain forests in Brazil. Emile's parents found the tributaries along the Amazon a terrific winter retreat. The locals did seem a bit, well, *primitive,* but — no bother — his parents adopted the when-in-Rome philosophy and held twelve of the primitives in full-time employ.

Everyone in Emile's generation has a tattoo. It's their form of self-expression. This is a popular thought passed on to them by their parents: express yourself. Everyone is interested in who you are. I admired how Emile could ask me a question and then relate a story about himself. This pattern began with the cursory question on how I got started, which Emile echoed with an anecdote about how his father settled a suit about a *People* magazine article that alluded to the sexual orientation of some A-list movie star. *So that's how you become a senior staff writer.* Zola would be so proud.

When he asked how I met my wife, Emile relayed a story about a British colleague who admitted to masturbating to a picture of my wife taken on a topless beach in St. Croix when she was eighteen. When he asked how I enjoyed working with one of the hottest young producers in Hollywood, Emile declared his admiration for a man with such refined taste. The producer's taste in white wine was "awesome."

Emile and his generation use the word "awesome" a lot. Everything is awesome. "Awesome" means "to be awed." Was Chimp Brad's taste in wine really awesome? Was Emile's new tribal band tattoo awesome? The Grand Canyon is awesome. The Pyramids are awesome. There was nothing awesome about fat, confident Emile.

Finally, he stopped asking questions altogether. He needed to text a friend:

here with guy who thru
glove thru chix window

Between thumb strokes he felt the need to relay the story about how he lost his virginity after seeing the movie where the kid fucks his mother's glove. After he climaxed, he and his partner couldn't stop laughing as they remembered how my character used the glove to break his girlfriend's windshield. "When the thumb deflated? That was *awesome!*"

I tried to visualize Emile's partner as Emile informed the waiter that he wanted another glass of white wine. Then he announced his departure for the bathroom. As Emile Samarjian turned toward the lobby, I wondered if he was gay. His entire generation seems so perfectly manicured, so androgynous. Didn't they invent the metrosexual? It's OK to be pretty. Overpriced clothes and manicures are just another way of expressing yourself. Experimentation is just another form of self-expression. His parents experimented with drugs — why can't Emile dabble in boys? I'll say one thing for my generation: people who are gay own it. No middle ground. Got to admire them for that. They choose a side and stick to their, um, guns. I wondered how Emile would be as a parent. Self-involved, narcissistic Emile. Could he forgo a day at the spa when it came time to buy books for his child? I suppose he could call his mommy and daddy for help. Isn't that what they told him on the family outing for matching tattoos? "You can always call us for help."

Whom would I call for help? OnStar. They would at least tell me where I was. They would tell me that I was in L.A. That I was in the Chateau Marmont Hotel. They would tell me that my room overlooked the bungalow where John Belushi died. They would tell me that I was minutes away from ending the interview with doughy, confident Emile. That there was a cozy place at the hotel bar with my name on it. They would tell me it was raining outside. That the construction on my house was almost two months behind. That the construction on the screenplay for *The Chihuahua in the Goddamn Bag* was six months past due. They would say that I should worry about the giant hole my contractor called the pool. They'd dug too close to the slope. OnStar would remind me that I lived in the Hollywood Hills. That my house faced the HOLLYWOOD sign. That, despite how unhappy I was, I was only hours away from a blissful night of sleep. Emile's parents would be proud of me. My bliss was sleep. I would know because OnStar would tell me so.

Young, confident, self-absorbed Emile was back. Who was he talking to? I admired his considerable multitasking skills. He must regularly watch Oprah, prophet of the multitasker. His cellular friend was a nipple to the world. As it is for his entire generation. They are addicted to noise. Generation Noise. Emile listened, talked, texted, and viewed "pix" and video all at almost exactly the same time. All with his right hand. His left hand surrendered the company plastic to pay the bill. I wondered if Emile had ever paid for anything in his whole life. He went from his parents' pockets to his expense account at *People.* Thank God for that A-list actor's questionable sexuality.

Emile is a good kid, don't get me wrong. His generation is selfish but kind. I don't even know how to explain it. He didn't say "thank you" or "excuse me." But you can't confuse the lack of politeness and manners for unkindness. He believes everyone is equal. His entire generation does. Emile has participated in scores of sporting events and has the trophies to prove it. There were no losers when he played, only winners. When he vacationed with his parents in Brazil, there were only winners. The young men who cleared the field of sugar cane so Emile could practice soccer were winners because they participated in the life of Emile. That's what his mother told him. She would know. She's in real estate. She drives a Range Rover. That's Los Angeles for you. Real estate agents drive $85,000 SUVs while teachers struggle to make rent. The empire will die at the hands of fat, tattooed Emile and his fat, jobbed, fuckhole parents.

Emile finished reading the last of his text messages and took a swig of his white wine. "My friends can't believe I'm here with you. You're, like, our hero. We always quote your movies. 'Daryl, have you seen my mink gloves?' 'Daryl, look here, inside my glove? What do you suppose that is?' 'I swear, Kimberly, you start that car, and I'm gonna throw this furry rock through your windshield!' *And then you did!* You are so awesome!"

The waiter returned with the check. Emile smiled as he signed for *People.* He winked at the waiter. Or was it the waitress. I really couldn't tell. That's Hollywood. At least, that's what the sign across from my house says.

I walked Emile to the valet. We shook hands and exchanged pleasantries. I told him how much I admired his story. Where he came from. Who he was. If anyone gave a shit about a staff writer at *People* magazine, I'd be the guy to write the article. I knew more about Emile Samarjian than he knew about me. What he knew about me had already been made up about me. I've filed a few lawsuits. Maybe that's how Emile got the brand-new BMW that arrived at the valet stand. And those perfect teeth. *How do they stay so white?*

White wine.

"Hey, I'm meeting some friends at the Whiskey Bar. You wanna join us? I should warn you, my friends Josh and Tyler do a pretty mean impression of you."

"I'll take a rain check."

"Are you sure? We're all going down there to watch that man who fell into that hole. My friend Ethan is the manager. Every time they show the map where the man is, he buys the bar a shot of Jaeger. Last night we had, like, eight shots. It was awesome!"

A man fell into a hole? Was it my contractor? Was the hole my pool, which OnStar would assure me was dug too close to the slope? Did the HOLLYWOOD sign fall into the hole?

I hoped that confident Emile climbed into his BMW and made his way to the Whiskey Bar and the man in the hole. I hoped he drank ten shots of Jaeger tonight. I hoped he had an awesome time. I hoped his friends Josh and Tyler did their impressions of me as they soaked paper napkins with white wine and tried to throw the wads through the windshields of their sexuality. I needed a drink. I needed Larry Forgettable's unforgettable handshake. I needed someone to give me hope. Confident, self-assured Emile climbed into his new car. The passenger window slid down. Hope had yet to spring eternal.

"Uh, Mr. Beale? Is there anything you'd like me to write about you? I mean — like, something nobody knows?"

Did I care what the readers of *People* knew about me? No. I couldn't give a shit. I shook my head and watched young, confident Emile drive off into the night. What I would have given for just one moment of his blissful ignorance. I turned back to the doors of my hotel. Maybe Larry Forgettable could help me forget Emile.

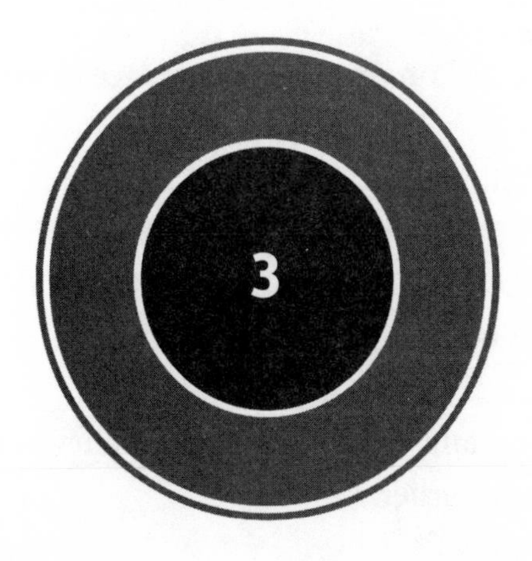

SOMEONE NOBODY KNOWS

The bartender-pharmacist refilled my prescription for red wine. A stand-up chap. If he's not careful, I may recommend him for employee of the month. He'll need a good black-and-white photograph that we can put up next to the register. Emile's last question has spurred a bit of a project. What would I want the world to know about me that it doesn't already know? I've already filled the back of one cardboard coaster, and I'm almost through a second. The project mirrors my wine consumption. It's amazing the amount of information you can fit on the back of a cardboard coaster.

I began with something most people know, unless they had seen me only in a magazine or on screen. Kind of like testing the water temperature with your toes.

- I am slightly above average in height but not in weight.
- I cheated on my college entrance exams.

There's a secret.

- I didn't lose my virginity until I was twenty years old.

Although in certain circles it is widely believed the event occurred six years earlier.

- I cried every day until my eighteenth birthday.

I have cried once since. One time in twenty-six years.

- I have one secret I will never tell anyone.

It's really not that big a deal. It's something I saw that I promised I would keep only for me.

- I have never been to see a therapist.

This despite the fact that I don't remember the last time I was happy. My grandmother didn't like me as a child. Which I discovered at the premier of my first movie. It followed this statement: "I'm just so proud of you — to tell you the truth, I never thought you would amount to anything." My grandmother raised me. My father was murdered. She always told me he died in a car crash. Turns out my father wasn't such a great guy. Guns don't kill people. Guns kill people who steal drugs from people who kill people with guns.

- My mother lives in a commune in Oregon.

The common belief is that she is an artist. My mother, in fact, is crazy.

- I have spent roughly $14,500 at Starbucks this year.

I will pass the $15,000 mark with the purchase of the Avrenches espresso machine — nickel-plated, dual-nozzle — a wedding gift for my wife's life coach, René. Almost every gift I give is from Starbucks. A favorite are those gift cards. They're easy and thoughtless.

- I cannot iron a shirt.

My inability to perform this most menial of tasks thoroughly pisses me off. I have been known to break valuable household objects while ironing. I will tell you I am a pacifist, but I'm angry about everything.

- I have had one homosexual experience in my life.

It was with a priest. It took me twenty-five years to realize it wasn't my fault.

• I lie. All the time.

The only time I'm ever honest is when I write. Yes, really.

• I do not love my wife.

I have never loved my wife. When the priest — a different priest — asked if I promised to love till death do us part, I lied. I am in love with somebody else. Her name is Zoë. Besides the occasional e-mail, I have seen her three times in thirteen years. She married somebody else. I secretly hope she is unhappy. I hate myself for that. I hate myself for a lot of things.

I looked at that word, "hate." I hate a lot of things, it seems. Why am I so angry? Why am I so mean? I wasn't always this way. I look up from my assignment. I can see my face in the mirror behind the bar. Larry Forgettable's eyes find mine in the reflection.

"I know. Sad, huh? I just think of his family."

Thank God for people like Larry Forgettable. What story does he want to recount this time? What's sad? Whose family? Is he referring to his latest brew of pit bulls? Will he take my suggestion and name the next litter after famous German war criminals? Who wouldn't want a dog named Goebbels or Himmler? "Hitler" is a little too on-the-head, but with his clientele he might be able to smuggle a Mengele through.

But there's no repetition in Larry today. His eyes focus on the television above the bar. The bartender takes up position next to him.

Larry Forgettable shakes his head. "Do you believe this shit?" A pause. "You think he's still alive?"

On the TV screen is a map. Is this the subject of Emile's drinking game? Yes. A man has fallen into a hole. From what I can gather, he is a family man. Married, two children, fifty-one years old. I wonder if he loves his wife. I wonder if he has any secrets. Did he cheat to get into college? Did he even go to college? Does he hate himself? What would he want soft, white Emile to write about him?

I feel for the man. Fifty-one years of obscurity, and his fifteen minutes come from the darkness of a hole. Fortunately the media has rallied the troops for continuous twenty-four-hour coverage. Lucky us. They even come up with catchy slogans as reporters report over and over again the same tired information. They find a man from Pennsylvania who works in a mine and ask him how other hikers can avoid such accidents. On-site grief counselors mollycoddle people who fear falling into similar holes or who are having a hard time processing the trauma. Some man with "reverend" in his name asserts that the hole represents the chasm between the upper class and minorities.

The entire group comes together in one big circus. One great big glorious circus. They call it "a media event." It's the ultimate in reality TV, exploiting what it does best — human tragedy. Historically there has been many a great media circus. There was the footballer-who-murdered-his-wife-and-her-friend circus. The moon-walking child-molester circus. The guy-who-murdered-his-pregnant-wife-so-he-could-have-an-affair-with-some-white-trash-masseuse circus. Some circuses are unfair. Like the handsome-president-who-got-blown-by-the-fat-girl circus. His problem was timing. He should have been president thirty years earlier. Everybody loved Dick in '68.

Larry Forgettable is awed. This is the best media event this year. His mouth hangs wide open. Maybe that's why he got that spider web inked on his neck. The flies he can't catch with his mouth he can certainly trap beneath his chin.

Four minutes to the handshake.

SLOW ASCENT IN HELL

The elevator at the Chateau Marmont is like a float at some satanic parade. This is especially true after last call. You get people like the ninety-pound girl with the hundred-pound tits. It looks like they hung a huge tray on a car at some fifties roller-diner. Her friend has lips that have a visible pressure gauge. She looks like a clown. I don't know where to focus. Should I suggest lip chick kiss tit chick on the tits? That way I can concentrate on both. What's with their male friend in the mesh tank? Sleeve tattoos? How about a simple shirt? Nice nipple piercings. What say I give one a tug to see if a raft shoots out your ass? Nice tattoo, Fat Girl. Very original. A butterfly rising out of the crack of your ass. Thank you. Thank you for ruining doggy style for me forever.

Uh-oh. The guy who looks like a U-boat commander recognizes me. Nice knit cap, Hanz. It's eighty-five degrees outside.

"Hey . . ." he says.

"Guten tag."

"What?"

When was the last time you were in an elevator with a U-boat commander who didn't speak German?

"You were in that movie where the guy fucks the glove," he says. "You're the guy who threw the glove with the limp thumbdick."

I look up at the floor register: *4 . . . 5 . . .*

"Hey man, what the fuck? Jus' 'cuz you're famous don't mean you get to ignore us. You're not private property. I pay your salary, man!"

Fat Girl totally agrees with Hanz. "Yeah, least you can do is acknowledge the compliment."

I force a smile. *Don't do it.* I stare at the register: *7 . . . Don't do it.*

Big Tits laughs under her breath. "Maybe he can't talk unless somebody writes what he's supposed to say."

Big Lips loves making fun of people she doesn't know. "He's definitely not as good-looking in person."

Ding! Ninth floor. I step into the hallway.

Mesh Tank has a thought. "Fuck this dawg, he only on the ninth floor. Shee-it, we kickin' it ol'-school, penthouse way."

I stop short. *Don't do it.* I turn to the elevator. *Don't . . .* OK, just don't hit anybody. You're on probation. Remember the papers after the fight in New York? The handshake is just down the hall. Follow your bliss. Emile's parents would be proud.

No, they would tell you to express yourself.

I block the doors from closing. Mesh Tank first. "News flash, Inkpad: you're white. Trying to be black insults the struggle of what it means to be a minority." Then Big Lips. "Fuck you, Mrs. Ed. Your lips belong under the seat of a plane. And Big Tits, you look like a monster truck. Twenty years ago you'd have been a missile silo in a Kansas wheat field. And there's nothing uglier on a fat girl than a tattoo. Wait, no, a U-boat commander on a fat girl. That's uglier. *Guten nacht.*"

I turn back to the hallway.

Big Tits proves the meanest and most creative of the group. "Fuck you, asshole!"

"Just don't shoot me with your tits."

The elevator continues on to the kick-ass urban party upstairs.

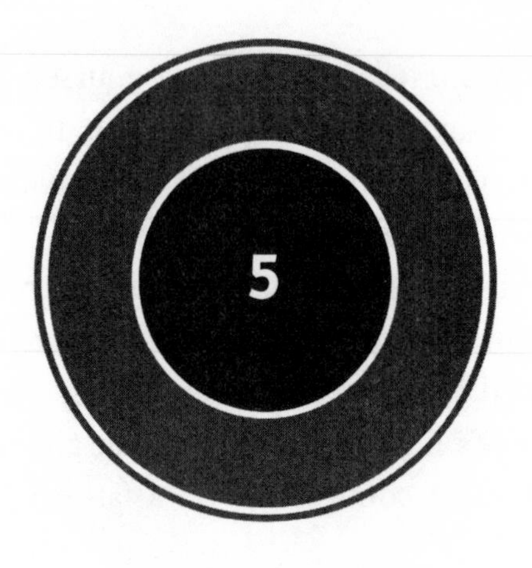

SHAKING HANDS UNDER THE YUM-YUM TREE

I settle comfortably into the westernmost of two queen-size beds. Two A.M. I have opted to forgo the single king after several "accidents" with the handshake. On day three, Rush Chairman Larry Forgettable gave me my directions and materials. On day forty, my local PayRite pharmacy supplies materials. The routine is now just that — routine. Two tabs of over-the-counter pain medication with "P.M." on the box, two tabs of over-the-counter allergy medication — no initials on the box — one capful of that late-night, sniffling and sneezing, so-you-can-rest medicine. Dutifully mixed with one glass red wine.

TV on, volume down, remote in hand, I slug down the last of the red. The man is still in the hole. I click through the axis of evil: CBS, NBC, ABC, FOX, CNN, CNBC, MSNBC, TBS. The whole circus is at the hole. Commercial. What are they selling around the hole? It's that ad with the tiny elves who make cookies under the giant yum-yum tree. My mind tries to focus. The handshake almost has me in its grip. It's only a matter of time. My mind wanders.

Why are there no minority elves under the tree? Only pristine Germanic, Nordic, and Anglican elves. Tiny, happy, blond-haired, blue-eyed elves. Why does it bother me? I have blue eyes. The Aryan elves carry large black, brown, and yellow chips on their shoulders and then drown them in white, wavy dough. Could the conspiracy decried by men with "reverend" preceding their names be right? Could it be that this global conspiracy has reached all the way to the American snack industry? This is huge. Epic. The snack is an American institution. No red-blooded, true-blue American could begin or end his day without some sort of sugary treat. Could the chips they smother in dough be metaphors for the chips on the shoulders of minorities? Isn't that what the soft, doughy white men in charge tell us? What would be so wrong with a Mexican elf? Under the big peyote tree making his own special taco-chacos, if you will.

"Taco-chacos," I mumble aloud, laughing at my own joke, a big, bong-hit laugh.

What would the black elf make? White elves uncomfortable. The Asian elf would open an eatery in Beverly Hills called Little Wang's.

My eyes roll to the back of my head.

Welcome to the hole.

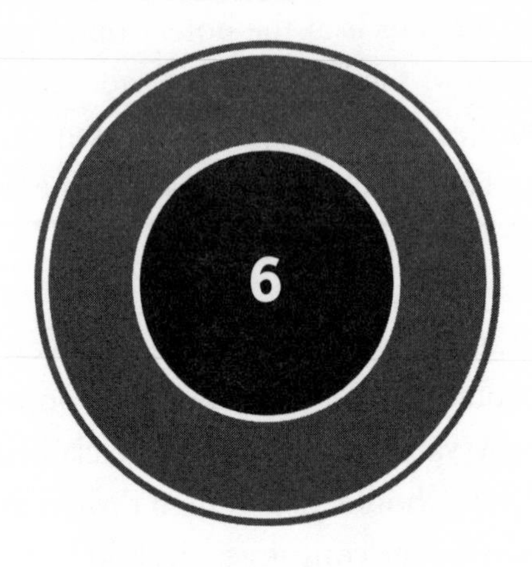

MORNING FOG AND BETRAYAL

I don't remember waking up. Seven A.M. I don't remember sitting in this chair. I don't remember dressing. The handshake usually affords ten solid hours of sleep. I kept my end of the bargain. Two tabs over-the-counter pain medication with "P.M." on the box. Two tabs over-the-counter allergy medication, no initials. One capful of that late-night, sniffling and sneezing, so-you-can-rest medicine. All dutifully mixed with the red. Why the betrayal?

The TV is still on, volume down. A graphic glows on the screen. A rock has given way and crushed a timber tie near where the man in the hole was lodged. He has fallen another forty-four feet. They've lost contact. Heavy fog surrounds the hole, hampering the rescue effort. Is he dead?

My arm is asleep. Did I sleep on it again? It burns as I open my hand. My Starbucks coffee card falls to the ground. Did I get up for coffee? Yeah, that's probably it. I couldn't sleep, so I got up for coffee. I wonder what the man in the hole would give for a cup of coffee. There's another map. Is Emile being betrayed? Have they stopped serving Jaeger? *Fuck, my arm hurts.* Maybe I'm having a heart attack. No chest pain, no shortness of breath. No history of heart disease. Just my arm and a brief bout of hypochondria. I reach down for my Starbucks card. *Coffee.*

I pull my hat low over my eyes as I walk into the hallway — on the off chance that the hundred-pound tits and the rest of the miscreants from the elevator are planning an ambush. Good news: not a silo or tat in sight. I wait for the elevator doors to open and introduce me to the stranger known simply as the morning person.

It's been a long time since I traveled with his kind. Morning people are an odd lot. They talk. They smile. They are usually drug and alcohol free. They are the captains that keep this great-big country of ours solidly steeped in the tradition on which it was founded: consumption. "Early to bed, early to buy" is their motto. They usually begin their day by connecting with their favorite personalities via the age-old television standard known as the morning show. Through the morning oracle they learn what's hot and what's not. They see the latest fashions, the hippest trends, their favorite celebrities. All in the privacy of their own little cocoons.

They sip hot beverages and eat unhealthy meals as they learn what's in store for them in the day ahead. *Is a new movie opening today? Was my favorite celebrity arrested for drunk driving while I slept? What make-up product do I want to buy? Yes, I do want to change my hairstyle.*

There are serious topics, too. How many people's children were killed in that war? You know, the one we're fighting to spread the joy of what it means to be American. Blood is red, but so are some of the stripes on our flag. Shouldn't every country in the Middle East have a morning show? Who wouldn't be happy watching *Good Day, Iraq?* If I lived in the Middle East, I wouldn't know the first thing about purchasing that hip new Christmas burka for my wife. That information I could glean only from my favorite morning-show anchor. There's a reason they call them anchors. They anchor our lives by showing us how to live.

Some morning people travel to see their favorite morning shows live. They stand outside in the rain, snow, sun, fog — just so they might glimpse the perky smile of their favorite morning-show personality behind safety glass. The morning person on vacation, that is whom I will encounter. This is a hotel. This is Hollywood. The most popular show tapes just up the street.

The doors open. Good news: five of them. Morgan Beale, meet the morning team. I step into the elevator and turn away from the crowd.

As a general rule of thumb, there is no talking or eye contact in an elevator. Unfortunately, the devils at Verizon, AT&T, and T-Mobile summarily dismissed this simple human contract, which was signed with the advent of Mr. Otis's machine so many years ago. The cell phone knows no arena that is off limits. Automobiles, bars, bathrooms, churches, department stores, grocery stores, liquor stores, restaurants, sidewalks, theaters — all are suitable cellular locations. Why should the elevator escape?

The voices surround me. The morning team is on the phone. Focus. Remember the man in the hole. Is he a morning person? No. He fell into the hole while walking at night. They interviewed his friends from his local bar. Good news: the man in the hole is a drinker! What does he do for a living? *Goddamnit.* Who are these people talking to? Emile? Emile's friends Josh and Tyler? And why is the conversation always the same? Discussions of relationships, clothing, movies, and television. Things they've learned from their morning-show gurus. They talk about the latest scandal, the diet they're on, the price of gas, music, their child's play date, and, luckily today, the latest media event. Five faces in the elevator with me. Five faces each talking to somebody somewhere else. A wireless moment shared from one hole to another.

"He must be half-starving to death."

You'd expect that comment from the fattest face in the lift. Whenever I ride in an elevator with a person of girth, I automatically find the posted weight capacity. Then I make hasty estimates — add up the numbers to see if there's any chance we might plummet to our deaths. No problem on this flight, thanks to the fat man's wife-and-daughter combo, Anorexia and Nervosa. They talk to other people about the man in the hole. Anorexia seems even more shallow than her daughter.

"Did you see the blouse the wife was wearing? What, she only shops secondhand?"

Rich people in elevators shouldn't throw stones. I envision Anorexia looking over at the nightstand clock as Big Daddy unloads in her, pumping away as she fantasizes about the tennis pro with whom she likes to have a glass of white wine after her weekly lesson. Wait, the daughter has a thought.

"Why don't they lower, like, a phone down there or something so he can at least have somebody to talk to?"

Nervosa isn't shallow — she's retarded.

"Our daughter is so thoughtful."

The other two faces between Tubby and Twiggy are Japanese tourists. Who knows what they're saying? Probably something about the man in the hole. I concoct an idea that, as Nervosa's eyes wash north from the Japanese tourists' shoes, above their pants and shirts, she will stop and focus on the couple's collective face. A light bulb, albeit a dim one, will illuminate over her head, and she will relay a clever idea. If they could just get a spoon to the man in the hole, he could dig his way to China. Good luck to her and her future career at Hot Dog on a Stick.

Nervosa cups her phone to her chest. "Mom, we have to *hurry.* At the top of the hour they're gonna do 'Style File.' They're gonna teach us how to dress like a Kennedy!"

Big Daddy smiles at his wife. She'd look great in a pillbox hat. He'd look great drunk with his pants around his ankles: "Big Teddy style," they'd call it.

"Say, Hal, what's the local station sayin' 'bout the new quarterback the Cowboys traded for?"

Now it makes sense. They're from Dallas.

"After the show, we're going into Beverly Hills. Ned wants to see the street from *Beverly Hills Cop.* Me? I just want one minute in Harry Winston's."

Killing them crosses my mind. Can you kill somebody who's already brain dead? Not in America. Only God can kill somebody who's brain dead. At least that's what that historical document you find in hotel rooms says.

The stupidity of this family is staggering. Thank God for the language barrier with my friends from the Land of the Rising Sun. I look at the emergency phone in the elevator. I pray for a call from the governor. *Ding!* They've heard my call. The elevator doors open, freeing me from death row.

Doorman Norman always winks at me. I always smile. Not because he winks but because I hear in my head *Doorman Norman, Norman the Doorman.* Whatever floats your boat, right? Doorman Norman says he loves every movie I've ever made. A lot of people say that. Truth is, most of them have seen only one of them. You know which one that is. Truth is, Norman and the morning people wouldn't like anything but *Gloveboy.* No tits, no ass, no movie stars who flip in the air before they kick an assassin to the ground. No explosions, no torture scenes, no model-spies with Ph.Ds. No rogue cops who jump cars into buildings, no serial killers, space aliens, or giant snakes. None is a remake of some great old movie or television show that reminds us of our youth. They're just stories. The first one was a story, too, and I'm sick of being reminded about it every minute of every fucking day.

I step through the hotel doors to take my place in the world of the morning people. How will I react to seeing my shadow opposite where it normally stands? Looks like I'll have to wait for an answer. There's no sun this morning. Fog in Los Angeles? Is this the same fog hindering the rescue of the man in the hole? But he's fallen in Pennsylvania. You'd expect fog in the hills where you'd find an old abandoned mine. Sunset Boulevard has no abandoned mines. The gold on Sunset Boulevard comes from the riches above the street. The movie stars, the fancy cars, the beautiful people with their perfectly sculpted features.

This doesn't mean there aren't holes on Sunset Boulevard. In fact, there are a few "holes" just outside the doors of the hotel. They would like to call themselves photographers, but their true name is paparazzi. "Paparazzi," from the Latin *papacornholefucker* and *razzispunkguzzler,* terms used in the early Catholic Church to refer to a man who is born with no vertebrae, which consequently allows him to spend his days admiring his own asshole. This is also where we get the phrase "He has his head up his ass." "Paparazzi" literally means "a guy with his head up his ass." This is why all paparazzi carry so much equipment. The bulk of the camera and attachments prevents not only the head but the entire body from sliding up said asshole, an act that would cause the paparazzo to disappear. Stephen Hawking would call it Black Hole Syndrome. I prefer to think of the ouroboros — the snake eating its tail.

Three holes follow me onto the sidewalk. They stay a safe distance away. You see, a lot of holes fear me. Seems I have a bit of a temper sometimes. It's really not me they want, anyway. They want my wife. Don't they watch TV? Hunter is in New York.

Of course they don't watch TV. They have their heads up their asses.

THE HUNTER

My wife, Hunter, likes to have her picture taken. As I pass the newsstand across the street from the hotel, I count at least nine pictures of her. Hunter shopping in SoHo, Hunter eating near the park, Hunter with mystery man. Rumor has it that Hunter and I are talking of separating. We separated three months ago.

What does *People* have to say about Princess? "Uncover the truth about America's favorite bad girl." What have the coconspirators of soft, androgynous Emile discovered about Hunter? What has been uncovered that hasn't already been written? Something nobody knows? I mean, so many wonderful things have been said about America's Princess. She loves animals. She loves her daughter, even though she sent her to live with her good-looking grandfather and chocolaty-rich grandmother. With Hunter's schedule, who has the time? Isn't that why she forgot her daughter in the VIP room at the Motorola party? Her demanding schedule? *Someone* had to walk the red carpet. Hunter isn't forgetful. So she did that bump of blow in the limo. That's why she had her daughter escorted to the VIP room — to shield her from the holes around the red carpet. The cocaine? Mommy just needs to let her hair down sometimes. It's better she's with Grandpa Handsome and Grandma Creamy anyway. No cocaine there. Just prescription pills and vodka. Don't worry, Hunter's little girl has her own little VIP room. She cries herself to sleep in it all the time.

If pressed, I would say that the only thing I love about Hunter is her daughter. The biggest fight I ever had with Hunter was when I suggested that Camille live with us. Hunter dismissed the idea with incident. Much incident. I understood her position, though. I wouldn't want to live in a house where two people hated me, either.

Here's something they don't know about America's sweet-tart. Precious likes to get beat up in bed. Her favorite position is missionary with a forearm pressed combatively across her neck. Then a bit of the rough rumpy-pumpy until her eyes roll back into her head. It's her own little secret handshake. Hunter likes to be slapped, kicked, burned. Hunter likes to be hunted. Tie her, trap her, chain her — extra brownie points if you take her down in one shot.

I know the mystery man. He's the man Hunter's been fucking for the last three years. I guess that's the price you pay for not beating your wife. He's a stunt man. She met him on a movie I was directing. When I first discovered Hunter's liaison, I tried to kill her stunt man by having him hit by a car. Scene 96 – JOGGER KILLED ON DESERTED ROAD. It wasn't in the original script I'd written, but I do have a reputation for changing things as I go along. Just a late-night rewrite, that's all. You know, to give the lead character a bit more gravitas. The stunt man bounced right back up — not a scratch on the bastard. If I'd had a gun on me, I'd have shot that silly I'm-fucking-the-slut grin right off his face. Maybe I'll have him pushed off a building in the *Dog in a Bag* movie. That'll teach him not to burn Hunter's nipples with cigarettes.

The three holes are still following me. I toy with the idea of simply telling them that Hunter is in New York, knee-deep in the urine of the mystery man. There's a picture for America's newsstands. Princess Hunter with piss hood, firmly clamped to a lawn spike. Why does that make me smile?

I need coffee, the antidote to the secret handshake. The antidote consists of four shots espresso, one-half cup nonfat milk, and the perfect topping of foam — all delivered in that cheery white beacon in a perfect brown sash, known to all as the Starbucks Venti. One-half block to the antidote.

I know it's hard to believe I would need to unwind after a night of "sleep," but mornings have been, for as long as I can remember, as foggy as the air today. I can honestly say I don't remember the last time I wasn't slowed by a hangover, however slight. I subscribe to the belief that a man should drink to hangover at least once a month just to remind himself that he's alive. Ben Franklin said that. Or maybe I read it in *Hustler.*

Either way, I am reminded every morning that I am alive. As for the handshake, a whole new set of problems has arisen. But at least I'm sleeping.

The three holes cross the street ahead of me. I am obviously a victim of my routine. They know my first stop is the paper stand on the corner. They are genuinely excited about the sudden time change of my daily pattern, which may bring some unexpected windfall. Hunter is a morning person. She said so in the book she wrote. Hunter loves the morning sunlight. What she won't confess is that the reason she's up so early has nothing to do with the light but the eight ball of ski she's gone through. The morning sun reminds her to take her downers. I grab a copy of the *New York Times.*

The man at the newsstand knows me now, thanks in part to my frequenting his shop for forty-one days straight. He didn't recognize me until a picture of Hunter and me appeared in one of the rags that grace the pearly-white gates of his establishment. I buy the same thing every morning: one *New York Times.* I used to read the *Los Angeles Times* until there was a discrepancy over a fourteen-dollar invoice that the liberal hierarchy at the big L.A. paper sent to a collection agency. When you are trying to buy the latest, greatest hybrid car for your wife to drive to her stunt man–disciplinarian-lover's home, the last thing you want to learn is that there's a lien on your credit. When my wife stormed out of the Honda dealership, I wanted to punch her in the mouth — but I didn't want her to take it the wrong way. The last thing anyone wants to do after they learn their credit is suspect is fuck.

I lay the necessary coinage on the counter.

"When you gonna bring that pretty movie star wife of yours by?" He smiles through the heavy acne scars on his cheeks. Who told him the gold tooth was a great fashion statement? Why the Mercedes medallion on a chain around his neck? Does he think he's a car? I force a smile. Why can't he fall into a hole?

I read the paper every day. I'm particularly fond of the obituaries. Not in a morbid way. I just want to remember the people whom the citizens of the United States of Consumption will never know. The people who gave them their SUVs, their disposable lighters, their cell phones with Bluetongue technology. All of the titans who gave them plastic, paper towels, and coffee sleeves. The artificial sweeteners, fast food. The genius of the TV remote and the reservoir-tip condom. The triple-action razor for that extra-close shave. Prepackaged meals, CDs, DVDs, and the cardboard boxes that make every product so appealing to the eye. These are the people who are dead today. Thank you, dead people.

As I make my way to Starbucks, I peek into my paper. I will avoid Arts & Leisure so as not to allow Hunter to ruin my new routine. I wonder if I'll like being a morning person. I pull the Arts & Leisure section free. Yep, there's Princess Kick Me on the front page. She's been bargain hunting in Chelsea. Seven hundred dollars for a clutch? What a steal!

Hey, holes, how's this for a picture? My wife and her new condom cozy into the garbage! *Booya!*

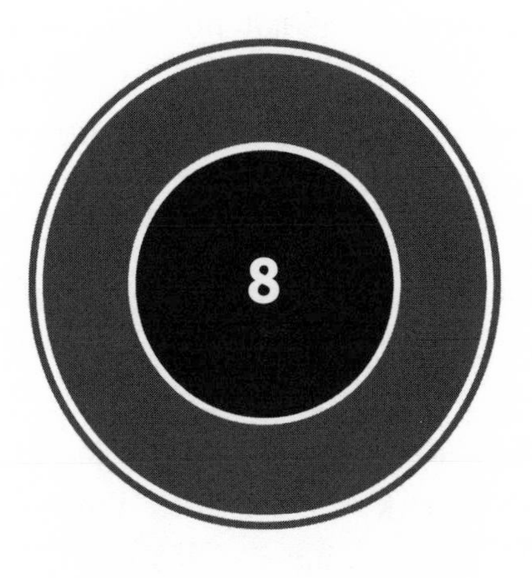

STARBUCKS NATION

The phone company is up early this morning, three trucks braving the morning rush. No traffic moving east or west means I am safe to cross against the red. The holes camp out on the corner. It offers a good vantage point to corner anyone coming or going. A team of phone-company employees dismantles a phone booth in front of the Starbucks. This is my forty-first day in this particularly handsome green giant. This is a flagship store. It has soothing raspberry walls, light maple tables, and a cheery bright stage where the baristas perform. Lost for a thought in Starbucks? Not in this store — printed musings float on the wallpaper and cups alike. Starbucks is America's national theater. Place your order and await a performance personally tailored for said request.

"Venti, half-caf, caramel macchiato for Richard!"

"Grande, nonfat café au lait, no foam, for Tracy!"

"Peter, your triple espresso is now on the bar!"

"Two-pump, decaf, nonfat, mocha Venti — NO NAME!"

"VENTI DRIP FOR BIG BILL!"

The phone company works in the enormous hole in front of my flagship Starbucks. I wonder to myself how many of these men would be interested in one of Larry Forgettable's pit bulls. Lots of moustaches, lots of body art. The chick in the hardhat has Target written all over her. Would her girlfriend like a dog with a shark's head? I watch the hardhats climb in and out of the hole. I wonder — if I climb beneath the asphalt, could I save the man in the hole? The man on every network. The man so many miles away. The man who fell an additional forty-four feet. The man with whom they've lost contact. The man who might be dead. I think of this faceless man as they walk the dismantled phone booth around the hole and lay it on the flatbed of the phone-company truck. I can't remember the last time I saw a phone booth assembled or disassembled. Starbucks has replaced the phone booth. If you need to make a call, Starbucks is the appropriate place to connect. If Clark Kent needed to change into Superman, he would do it in a Starbucks bathroom. He would do all of his *Daily Planet* work in Starbucks, too.

Then, just when you think you've seen it all, the geniuses of industry give you a whole new mousetrap. Rising from the sidewalk, waiting to be introduced into the very spot of the soon-to-be-extinct phone booth, is a beautiful, deep-green monolith. Starbucks Nation and the powers that be are introducing the world to a whole new kind of vending experience: the Starbucks drink dispenser, a soda machine willing to bleed Starbucks goodness into the hands of Fat America everywhere. Now you don't even have to go inside and talk to another human being to retain that girth we Americans parade so proudly. Children can roll up on their sneakers, look back at their proud parents, and say, "Mommy, can I have a Starbucks treat to wash down my Ritalin?"

Mommy will smile. "Of course you can, sweetheart."

First the Starbucks drive thru, now this.

The Starbucks team works with the phone-company team. I wonder whether there will be an obituary in the *Times* for the phone booth. Will they reminisce about how the booth gave us our own little cocoons of privacy? Where people could see in and out but not hear in and out? Will they say the phone booth had outlived its stay in a world where self-importance is now king? Where it's people's inherent right to have their conversations erode the peace and quiet we experienced in the primitive age? I walk past the machine and into the flagship store.

At least twenty-five people are standing in line ahead of me. This is a particularly busy Starbucks, and, owing to the heavy foot traffic, a substantial work force has assembled to keep everything moving smoothly. At least twelve baristas are smiling. The baristas sport manifold tattoos and multiple body piercings. They have hairstyles like cornrows and dreads. They are liberal, androgynous, and get free coffee. They always seem to be smiling. Is the secret the free coffee? When you listen to them talk to each other, it's usually about music, TV, or movies. They rarely talk about war, politics, or religion. Yet they still wear religious symbols and buttons with peace signs or slogans espousing the folly of war. They are fond of statements like "no worries" and "it's all good." Baristas get free health insurance. This leaves extra cash for that old VW van with the broken muffler and the "Free Tibet" bumper sticker.

Baristas differ from the Emiles of the world. This is due in part to the chasm between their respective paths. It's true that the baristas' parents love them as much as the parents of Emile love him. However, baristas usually come from broken homes. Their parents are substantially younger than the doting souls who sired Emile. They didn't have the resources to give their little baristas-to-be that top-notch education or that all-important trust fund. While Emile received a car and an allowance, the baristas rode their skateboards through adolescence with little guidance. Emile has a discreet tattoo he can hide beneath his white collar, while baristas show little discretion in this area. There is no mystery to baristas. They wear on their sleeves who they are. Tattoos are their trust funds. Most will never own homes, know their credit scores, or plan for retirement. Emile will hang art in the new condo his doting parents will buy him while baristas will hang art on their bodies. They live now. No worries; it's all good.

Starbucks is a people zoo. It's an ideal place to observe the great experiment. I keep my baseball cap low so I can watch from the shadows.

A man in the corner tapping at his computer talks loudly on his cell phone. Starbucks is so much more than just a phone booth; it's a personal workstation. He laughs loudly. His workstation is a happy one.

Four women and a man cluster around another table. They meet for coffee before their Mommy & Me class. The mommies bounce their little cherubs on their knees. They all have tattoos on the smalls of their backs. They all project that perpetual "Look what I made with my vagina!" smile. Their husbands are agents and producers and lawyers. The single man-mommy stares down at his baby in its seven-hundred-dollar stroller. His smile is suspect. Does his wife know he likes white wine?

I feel light-headed, and my arm is still asleep. I also have substantially more random thoughts than usual. The morning after the secret handshake usually brims with more fog than thought. Seems the fog in my head has leaked outside to the streets of Hollywood. There's a lot more noise in this Starbucks than I remember. My eyes continue moving from table to table.

Four suits at that table: three men, one woman. They all talk on cell phones to somebody else. The woman suit cradles her cell phone on her shoulder as she reads a message on her BlackBerry. She shows the text to an older suit across the table. He nods approvingly. She sets the BlackBerry down. With one hand free, she can finally relax. She can keep one hand plugged in to the world, with the other plugged in to that twice-a-week sex partner with the occasional scented candle. Maybe she'll try anal this week — they have been together a year.

At another table, an interracial couple holds hands. Just

one hand each. His free hand holds a cell phone. She's tapping at her iPod, her mind racing. She thinks of that new tattoo, her college boyfriend, the indiscretion with the sorority housemother, her black boyfriend she couldn't possibly take home to her parents in Wisconsin.

Everyone plugs in to something else. A girl has stopped in the middle of the sidewalk. Her thumbs pound away. How dare her boyfriend text her like that? Faces on phones, faces with earphones, faces looking anywhere but ahead — all move around the angry girl's world. Faster and faster they move. Nobody even notices the beautiful new green machine that will make their very important lives so very much easier to navigate.

"Hello, and welcome to Starbucks!" says my own personal barista. A Venti cup appears in front of his cheery, androgynous smile, delivered by a person whom I really couldn't identify one way or the other. S/he smiles "their" very happy, completely insured smile as s/he runs their tongue over the rings in their lower lip. "Four-shot, nonfat latte with regular foam — just like you like it. See? I remembered."

I reach inside my jacket for my wallet. The Lip begins rambling.

"I finally saw it. The one where the cute boy does it with his mom's glove? My boyfriend and me totally almost peed our pants when you smashed that windshield!"

As s/he talks there comes over me the most profound feeling of anxiety I have ever had. I look across at the smiling faces, a look of complete bewilderment on mine. "My phone . . . I forgot my phone . . . my wallet . . . I forgot my . . ."

The baristas smile. "No worries." One pokes his hands into the tip jar. "It's all good." The good, smiling hands of a barista pay for the antidote.

I can't breathe. Terror level elevated. Orange. Maybe even red.

"I'm not plugged in. Nobody knows where I am. I can't tell people where I am," I say, as if not being in touch with the great Wi-Fi gods in the sky is somehow a matter of national security. Whom will I talk to when I'm bored? Whom will I talk to when I work? Whom will I talk to while others are trying to talk to me?

I don't say thank you. I need to get out of here. I leave for the hotel, stepping past the big green Starbucks machine, around the hole, and into the street. *I need my phone.*

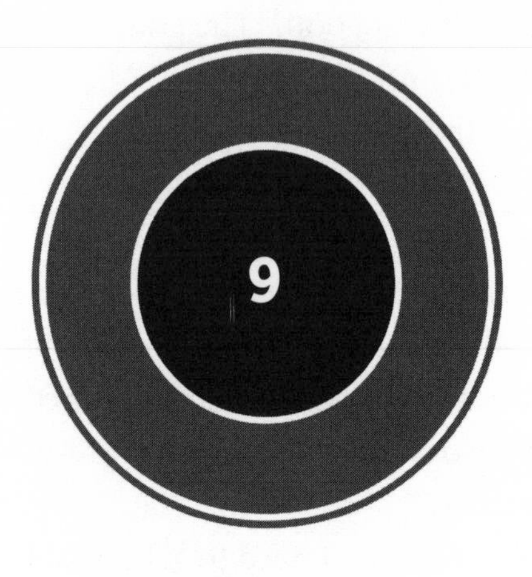

A GRAVE SIGHTING

I didn't get very far. My eyes stopped short: a hearse parked where the phone-company truck had been. Were they finally giving the phone booth a proper burial? Then a voice so startled me that I actually stumbled backward and dropped my Venti, four-shot, nonfat latte with that perfect dose of foam. It was a familiar voice, a voice I hadn't heard in years. Stepping out from behind the hearse was an old friend of mine. He moved through the fog and hopped onto the hood of the big black death wagon.

I have written twenty-seven screenplays, of which nine have been made into films. Of the twenty-seven scripts, on only three did I collaborate with another writer. They were the first three scripts I ever wrote. The first being the famous one of which I am reminded every day. That other writer is the man on the hearse. His name is Luke. He taught me how to write. It was Luke who directed my one and only scene. Luke made me famous.

Luke comes from a long line of writers. His grandfather was nominated for three Oscars, with one win in the late forties for a picture that swept the awards. His father was a multiple Emmy winner for one of the most-watched miniseries in television history. His mother wrote, among others, the definitive book on contemporary psychoanalysis.

I met Luke when I was twenty-eight years old, that is to say, sixteen years ago. He was thirteen years — almost to the day — older than I was. I was doing stand-up comedy at a tiny little club on the Sunset Strip. A mutual friend took him to the show. Luke was looking for a new writing partner with comedy skills. Luke liked to say that he wasn't very funny, which of course was bullshit. He'd say he was lazy; he needed someone around to push him into the pit, so to speak. That was bullshit, too. Fact was, Luke just liked to have fun, and writing's a lot more fun when it's not just you at the typewriter. When we thought up that glove smashing the windshield, his wife ran out to the garage because she thought we were torturing her cat with pliers. When she got there, she couldn't figure out how two seemingly healthy men could possibly both swallow their tongues at the same time.

I loved writing with Luke. We laughed. All the time. Luke taught me to be cool. How to fake it when you're scared they might find out you're a fraud. He taught me how to fake it around people like Hunter, the real frauds who rely on their money and self-esteem. He taught me how to dress, how to take over a room. He taught me how to meet girls — and when I found a little of the self-esteem my childhood had taken from me, he introduced me to Zoë.

Luke had been dead for thirteen years. A drunk driver killed him on Mulholland Drive. It was February 9, three days after his forty-fourth birthday. Yet there he sat, on the hood of a hearse. I couldn't move. Luke looked down.

"I think they've dug it too close to the hill."

"What?"

"Your pool. I think they've dug it too close to the hill."

I looked down at the hole where the phone company had been working. The shape and depth had changed. It looked remarkably similar to the hole in my backyard. It was very deep at one end, the shallow-end incline rising up to create a ramp into the cavity. The hearse sat at the top of the ramp, its headlights haunting the deep end of the hole.

Luke looked down at the hearse. "Wanna go for a ride?"

He looked at me with that same smile I remember from the day I threw the glove: warm, paternal, safe. "Come on, let's see how deep the hole is."

I stood motionless for a moment, then started for the car. I walked past the passenger-side door. I wasn't sure why, but it felt like I should ride in back where the coffin went. I heard the engine turn over as the passenger-side window rolled down. Luke leaned across the seat and called out, "Hey!"

I turned to the door as Luke pushed it open.

"You're not dead. Ride up here."

The leather felt cold. I pulled the door closed as the fog around the hole grew thicker. I couldn't see the storefront of the flagship Starbucks anymore. Visibility zero. Luke put the death coach in gear.

"Fasten your seat belt. God knows how deep this fucker is."

I pulled the seat belt across my lap. The fog outside began to fall into the hole, as if it were being sucked inside. He looked back then gunned it. The hearse flew down the makeshift ramp. My hands shot for the dashboard. *Panic.* We dropped into the deep end of the pit. It felt like the first great dip on a roller coaster — the feeling of being out of control yet knowing it was only a ride. The hearse pulled and jerked at breakneck speed. Luke was screaming not from fear but that elated scream you would associate with such a rush. I didn't scream. I couldn't.

We raced into the black. The hearse banked hard to the left as we accelerated into what looked like a horizon of computer code. Numbers, symbols, letters randomly arranged. Now it was all around us, the green hue of code on black. Code as a wall of light in the sky. The bright cipher rolled as if it were looking for some secret combination. The hearse banked hard to the right and dropped down below the horizon. I looked up. The code had fallen in on itself, creating one single line that raced around the edge of the void like the crawl you find on every news and sports program. I began to see words, numbers, symbols, all hiding within the code: today's date, news, names, information. My eyes couldn't take it all in. Then, a story I remembered. The man in the hole.

"He is forty-four years old. He cried every day until his

eighteenth birthday. His wife could not be reached for comment. He is in love with another woman." Wait, that was the wrong man. They were writing about the wrong man. He was fifty-one. He was happily married with two kids. "He cheated on his college entrance exams. His father was murdered. He lies." The hearse rolled over on its side, the crawl no longer visible.

Luke laughed. "I thought you said you lost your virginity when you were fourteen. Man, you really do lie about everything."

The joyride accelerated as the hearse rolled right side up. We blew past images on enormous screens. It was like riding the air above Times Square. Hunter's face flew by on both sides. Her friends, my friends. Every passing face on a cell phone, BlackBerry, iPod. Every face sipping Starbucks. Every face plugged in. Voices all around.

"Hey, I'm probably gonna lose you — I'm getting on the subway. Are you there? Hello? *Hello?*"

"Hey, me again. So anyways, I couldn't believe we found parking."

"He did? She *didn't!* . . . I'll probably wear something casual."

"I got the most beautiful distressed T-shirt at that boutique on Fifth — a hundred twenty dollars. I know, can you believe it?"

"No, I just sat down to lunch. You talk, I'll slurp."

"Doctor says it's erectile dysfunction."

"Damn retard thinks he's Jesus."

"Just got out. It blows. That fat critic was right."

Then an unexpected dip, and suddenly we were headed straight down. My hands gripped the dash. Luke was laughing uncontrollably. What first felt like a joyride had abruptly shifted gears. We no longer felt on track. We were falling. Blackness raced past us. Then, as quickly as it began, it stopped. The hearse pulled back up and settled on its wheels, the headlights focused on nothing. Luke beat his hands on the steering wheel.

"GOD DAMN! GOD DAMN! MOTHER FUCK GOD-DAMN WAS THAT WILD!" He faced me, smiling maniacally as he opened the door. "Let's check out the bottom of this hole."

He climbed out into the dark, crossed in front of the hearse, and stood bathed in the glow of the headlights. He waved me out of the car. "Come on."

I slowly opened the door as Luke crossed out of the light and disappeared.

"Hey, don't . . . where . . . Luke? *Luke?*"

Nothing. I couldn't even hear him. He'd disappeared. I stepped to the front of the car. I looked right, left, behind, up. No light from the crawl, no light from the monitors. Nothing but the void. Nothing but the deep, dark black of the hole.

LIGHTS, CAMERA, INACTION

How long had I been standing in front of the hearse? The headlights were dangerously close to going dark. A dead battery was our greatest enemy. How would we get home? As I processed this simple fear, the lights of the death coach died. It was like a cave; I could see nothing. I held my hand out in front of my eyes. I might as well have just disappeared. Was I dead? No. If I had died, I would have ridden in the back of the hearse. He said I was alive; Luke said I was alive. That was why I rode in the front.

Luke's voice called from above, through a megaphone, "Can I get some light on the writer?"

Suddenly light washed over me. I shielded my eyes. A shadow raced by, and I spun around.

Again Luke on the megaphone: "Bring the lights up on the set."

The familiar sound of a voltage switch. Followed by another and another. The hum of electricity. Light began to wash behind me, bright light, like the sun. Luke's shadow slowly descended from the sky. Was he flying? Was he on a wire? His figure shielded the light from above. He was sitting on the black leather stool of a film crane. He leaned against the camera.

"You'll never guess what's at the bottom of this hole."

He motioned to the light behind me. I turned, and my jaw hit the floor.

There it was. Starbucks. But not just any Starbucks: the flagship Starbucks. My flagship. In front of the store stood the green monolith, the Starbucks vending machine, proudly guarding the home of the antidote. I stared in at the warm raspberry walls, the comforting maple tables and chairs. I thought of all the cheery phone calls you could make inside, the text messages that would bring smiles. I longed for my nonfat, four-shot latte with that perfect dollop of foam.

Luke swung down in front of me. "What do you think?"

"It's a Starbucks." I was clearly confused.

"No, it's *your* Starbucks!"

I moved closer to the store. "Why?"

Luke and crane swooped to the other side of my shoulders. "We need a setting."

"For what?"

Luke's left eyebrow arched ever so slightly. I had forgotten he could do that. That always meant mischief.

"We're gonna write a movie."

You know that feeling you get when somebody wakes you from a deep sleep? You just can't process what anyone says. What movie? Was this a movie set? Was I directing the movie? No, I was the writer. He asked for light on the writer. This was Luke's set. He was the director.

"We're gonna have a laugh again. A big ol' fuck-mommy's-glove laugh. A goddamned smash-the-slut's-windshield laugh."

I smiled. A real smile. Probably the first time I had really smiled in years. It was definitely the first time in a long time I had smiled at the thought of that scene we filmed so many years ago. It was OK that Luke reminded me of it. It seemed right, honest. It was as if I was finally awake. Like I'd just climbed out of bed after a long night's sleep. I focused on Luke's face, another smile creeping to my lips.

"There it is! See? You do want to laugh again!" he said.

I did want to laugh again. It had been such a long time since I really laughed. Luke waved up at the light. He went to the megaphone.

"Props? Props! *PROPS!*"

Luke peeked out from behind the megaphone. His eyes focused on a spot in front of the Starbucks machine. Then he seemed to see something he had overlooked. He turned back to the dark with his megaphone.

"Sorry, my mistake."

He turned the megaphone a hundred eighty degrees to his left and barked, "Can I get some light on the desk?"

A spotlight illuminated a small, wood-plank table you

might find in some faraway country kitchen. It sat directly in front of the Starbucks drink dispenser. There was a single chair behind it. I knew this table. This was my table. This was my desk. This was where I wrote.

"Drop me to the floor," Luke called into the dark.

The crane dropped to ground level in front of me. Luke fished out three books from the cradle where directors store shooting scripts. He climbed off the crane and laid the books out with a wry grin.

"I even got your books."

When I write I always keep three books on my desktop: *Roget's International Thesaurus,* the *Oxford English Dictionary,* and the *World Almanac.* All accounted for. Luke turned back for the crane. His hand waved for me to follow.

"You haven't seen the best part. Come on."

He sat down on the seat of the crane, watching me. I approached cautiously. His voice hurried me along. "Come on!"

He grabbed hold of my forearm, pulling me onto the crane and into the seat normally occupied by the cameraman. He called through the megaphone, "Take us up."

The crane rose some forty feet in the air. The bright lights of the flagship Starbucks and the calming green of the vending machine glowed below.

Luke went to his megaphone. "Cue the lights on the scrim."

Again the whir of electricity. Switch after switch was thrown. Little pockets of light emerged. My head turned from pocket to pocket. Then, one pocket in particular grabbed my attention: the HOLLYWOOD sign, fully illuminated.

My eyes tracked from the infamous sign to the flagship Starbucks. I suddenly knew where I was. The flagship Starbucks stood on the site of my Hollywood Hills home. The view from the front of the store was the view from the rear of my house. My desk stood in the very spot it occupied in my office at home.

"Check out the hearse," Luke said.

The big black death wagon sat in front of the store, where the hole my contractor referred to as "the pool" had been dug. There was no pool. Yet.

"You think we parked too close to the hill?"

Luke through the megaphone: "Cue the hole!"

The ground around the hearse began to shake, slowly at first. Like an earthquake in the desert, the ground began to collapse, a slow movement as earth slid into an ever-increasing dark hole. It was the same hole we'd driven into. A shallow end operating as a ramp to terra firma rose from the menacing pit. Calm gave way to a sense that the bottom had finally fallen out. The hearse slid from the shallow end and was quickly sucked into the void.

Luke through the megaphone: "It's official; we parked too close to the slope. Take us down."

The crane descended to the floor of the sound stage. Luke motioned me off. "You wanna shoot it?"

"Shoot what?"

"The script."

"But we don't have a script."

"We'll wing it. This is Hollywood. We can't let not having a script slow us down. Nobody thinks about story anymore.

What America wants is sound bites! Fuck details! Story is dead. The story takes place in the Hamptons? We'll make it Malibu. Let's face facts; a golden retriever is a lot better than a Chihuahua. Who didn't love *Old Yeller?*"

He was mocking me. Nobody thought story was more important than Luke. He was teaching me a lesson. I'd sold out. I was the unoriginal thinker.

"Cue fog," he said.

Fog rolled from beneath the floor of the sound stage. It crept slowly along the ground and smothered everything in its path, including the Starbucks. The bright green lights of the vending machine and the warm lights in and outside the store cast a ghostly glow. Luke continued: "Morgan, go stand by the big Coke — coffee thing."

I stepped onto the sidewalk outside the flagship Starbucks.

Luke called from above: "Hey, remember the guy who fell into the hole? He died. It's all over the news. Sad that some people get their fifteen minutes but never get to enjoy them. They'll make a movie, and everyone will hear his name, but him? — nothin'. No talk shows, magazines, or newspapers, no movie premiers or fancy parties. Just six feet of dirt. You know, what gets me is that there is a whole hell of a lot of people in the hole, and what do you hear about them? Nothin'.

"Roll sound. Morgan! Get up next to the machine. Jeeze, for a guy who makes movies you sure don't take direction well."

I felt sad for the man in the hole. And Luke was right. What about all the people in holes we never hear about? I made for the vending machine. The fog was thickening.

"Got any change?" Luke asked.

"Change?"

"For the machine. I'd like to give you a bit of business. Product placement. Anyway, I think a can of one of those soothing Starbucks coffee beverages will help you take your head out of the game. You can sip it while you say your lines."

"I don't have any lines."

Luke swept in from above, fog splitting and swirling around him. He looked like a madman. His eyes peered through the viewfinder of the camera. "Write some."

He looked up glibly at the fog, his hands waving through the muck. The more he waved, the more it swirled. "Gettin' kinda foggy, isn't it?"

He reached into his pocket and pulled out a handful of coins. He poked through the change, looking for something in particular. There — lint. He cleaned up his palm and looked down at me. "What's it say it costs?"

I looked at the machine. There were no instructions. "It doesn't."

Luke offered a handful of coins. "Just keep feeding it till we make contact." Then he motioned for one of the coins back. "Wait, wait . . . Give me that big silver one back."

I handed back the largest coin. The crane rolled past me and across the front of the Starbucks. Luke steadied himself above the darkest part of the hole, some twenty feet away, and tossed in the coin.

Silence.

We both waited to hear the coin hit bottom.

Nothing.

Luke broke the long silence. "Wow, that's a deep hole. You

know, when you think about it, this hole is teeming with metaphor. Change disappears into the hole. It's the American way. Gonna go on that diet. Gonna change. Gonna change my life. A few days, maybe a month. Feel good about yourself, get on the scale. You gained two pounds. Fuck it — I'm gonna eat that pie. You spiral from there. Change disappears into the hole. I don't want to drink anymore. I have an alcohol problem. Off the sauce. One week, two weeks, two months. Boss promotes somebody else. You call your old friend, Mr. Bottle. Your liver falls into the hole. Gonna go back to sch —"

"Can I put the money in the machine?" I interrupted.

Luke rambled. Often. He liked to lay it on thick. Not a fan of "less is more," his motto was, more or less: "Give me an inch, and I'll take it for miles." He'd have made one hell of a southern preacher. The only way to move him on was to move him on.

"Sorry, digressing. Forgot how you hate that. All right, let's shoot this bitch."

Luke swung out of view. I loaded coins into the slot until a light above it blinked: "Make Your Selection."

"How we doin' down there?"

"It says, 'Make Your Selection.' "

Luke's voice came out of the dark. No megaphone this time. It was like he was right beside me. It was the confident voice of the director I remembered from my scene with the glove. I was on safe ground.

"All right, here's what I'm thinkin'. You make a selection, reach in, and pull the Starbucks goodness into your hands. You take a long look at the can, smile, then open that bad boy up. Take one sip and remark how lovely it is and how lucky we are to have something like Starbucks in our lives."

"Is this a commercial?"

"No."

"Sounds like a commercial."

"You wanna pull the can out and throw it in the hole?"

"No, I'd rather have the caffeine."

"That's what I thought. So open the can, take a sip, and say something funny."

Luke brandished the megaphone. "Roll sound. Speed. Camera. And . . . ACTION!"

I turned to the machine and made a selection. That is, I pushed the only button flashing. There was a whir, then the sound of a mechanism at the top of the machine. I followed the sound of something that seemed much heavier than a can. At about the middle of the machine, where the can or bottle would normally descend, was an opening larger than normal. It was actually a little higher than where the traditional opening would be. I waited for the antidote's proxy. A typewriter fell into view, an IBM Selectric.

"What happened?" Luke called.

"It dispensed a . . . typewriter. Your typewriter."

"*What?*"

I pulled the machine from the vending slot. The electrical cord trailed like an umbilical cord into the cubbyhole from where the typewriter appeared. It looked like the machine was plugged in to the Starbucks dispenser itself. I set the typewriter on my desk. I arranged the cord so that it ran around my chair, across the floor, and into the cubby. My chair sat two feet from the machine, so that if I leaned back on two chair legs, I could balance myself against it.

Luke descended. "My *baby!* I loved that typewriter! Look at the lines. God bless the geniuses at old-school IBM. Now everyone's on a computer. Every retard thinks he's a screenwriter just 'cause he bought some fancy software that says he's a screenwriter."

I looked at the typewriter, now an extinct dinosaur like its friend the phone booth. I poked at the keys. They snapped to attention. I remembered the machine fondly. I remembered taking turns behind the keys as we wrote the movie about the lonely boy and his mother's glove.

Luke swung beside me. "Let's put some paper in daddy's baby."

"It didn't come with paper."

"I put some on the table. It's under your dictionary."

I picked up the book. Beneath lay a stack of blank typing paper.

Behind my desk I was comfortable. Behind my desk I was at ease. Behind my desk I was at peace with the world. I positioned Luke's typewriter in front of me. I reached for a single sheet of typing paper and loaded it into the carriage. I remembered how the physical act of loading paper was a ritual I loved. It reminded me of possibility. I was God in this world. I began with a blank slate. I was the creator, Whim and Imagination my guardian angels.

"Hey, what should —"

The fog had become so dense I could barely see the typewriter anymore. The flagship Starbucks and the machine weren't visible at all.

"Luke?"

Nothing. I was alone in the fog, which continued to thicken.

"Hey, Luke! LUKE!"

No sound. Just fog. Then a cell phone broke the silence. A woman's voice answered the call.

"Hello?"

It was Hunter's voice.

"Hey, baby . . . you *nasty.* . . . My ass is still sore from last night. I can't. . . . I told him I'd call around five. It's his birthday. I don't know — maybe I'll talk dirty and let him give himself, like, a sympathy hand job or something. Hey, I know — you wanna come over and tie me up while I talk to him? You can spank me while he wanks himself."

Today was my birthday. I'd forgotten. Forty-four. One year for every extra foot the man in the hole fell. The dead man in the hole. Then a recorded voice. "You have — one — new message."

A beep followed by a voice. Zoë's voice.

"Morgan? Are you there, Morgan? Pick up the phone, Morgan. I wanted to say happy birthday. I don't know if you're in L.A., but . . . call me. I miss talking to you. I've been going through some stuff lately. I know you're busy. Anyway, happy birthday. I saw your picture in *People.* You don't look forty-four. It was good to see your smile." *Click.*

Smile? Profound sadness washed over me. Breaking the

silence surrounding the sadness, a phone rang, followed by another and another. The air filled with hundreds, maybe thousands, of ringing phones. Light pierced the fog from above. Was it lightning or just the images below the crawl above? Then the voices started.

"He said he needed space. . . . Right? Can you believe that?"

"No, we can't go to Hinano. Madison's ex still bartends there."

"There's a sale at City Lites — those slip dresses are, like, fifty percent off!"

"Are you happy with your current long-distance provider?"

"Oh, it's my prostate again. You'd think that doctor would keep wine in his office with all the glove work he does."

"Summer had both nipples done. Not the heavy-gauge or anything."

"No, I'm not doing anything. I'm in line at Starbucks. Hold on — Venti, nonfat, half-caf latte — OK, I'm back."

"What are you wearing?"

"It was that fuck face, Liam — Hey, I gotta go. Some chick thinks she's special 'cause she's got kids. Fuck you, bitch, it's my bank, too!"

"I don't know — Bill wants me to go with the D cups, but I'm afraid it'll ruin my routine on the StairMaster."

"Fuck, I gotta go — I just hit a Toyota."

The ring tones and voices were deafening. As one voice ended, another phone began ringing. I covered my ears.

Wind began to swirl around me, the voices and ringing growing louder and louder until they became static, meaningless white noise. The bright flashes of light bled through my eyelids. An enormous clap of thunder sounded. The fog became a funnel cloud. The white noise was pulling into the twisting mass. The wind pulled hard at the fog, creating a spout that moved toward the hole. The hole was operating like a giant vacuum. The funnel began to disappear at an alarming rate. Faster and faster into the abyss until there was nothing left.

Silence.

Calm.

Then another recorded voice.

"If you would like to make a call, please hang up and try again. If you need help, please hang up and dial your operator."

WIDE AWAKE IN THE MIDDLE OF THE NIGHT

It felt like the middle of the night, but I was wide awake. My head hadn't felt this clear and lucid in years. I felt uncluttered, unburdened.

I looked out over the Hollywood Hills and the bright lights of the HOLLYWOOD sign. Disentangled from its grip, I saw its beauty for the first time. The silence gave me a sense of serenity and peace.

I rose from behind the desk and made for the lot in front of the flagship Starbucks. The lot that was in the place of my backyard. But no sooner did I step in front of my desk than the entire set disappeared. I stared out at the blackness. The only thing that didn't disappear was my desk. As I moved back behind it, the set reappeared. I repeated my movements — two times, three times, four. Every time I got up from my desk, this world disappeared. As long as I was seated behind the desk with the typewriter in front of me, what lay before me existed. Otherwise it did not. Furthermore, when I stood in the dark in front of the desk, I couldn't think. My head became as foggy as the set had been. I stared down at the blank page in the typewriter. The machine began to type on its own.

FADE IN:

EXT. FLAGSHIP STARBUCKS — NIGHT.

A noise came from the shadows on the other side of the hole. There was something out there. Something in the dark. I could hear it moving.

"Luke?"

Out of the dark stepped a small Chihuahua. He was wearing a blue cardigan. As the dog came closer, I recognized it: Mr. Bobo, the dog from the book I was adapting, the dog in the designer handbag.

"Mr. Bobo?"

The dog moved closer. Then I heard Luke's voice. "Mr. Bobo . . . What kind of name is Mr. Bobo? I swear to God, if a dog can fit in a purse, they saddle it with the most inane name. Chi Chi. Muffin. Tiny. What would be so bad with Bob? Can you change it to Bob? If you can change the setting to Malibu, seems you should be able to lop off a vowel at the end of the name."

I looked up into the darkness. Luke was up there somewhere. "This isn't funny, Luke."

Mr. Bobo stared me down. "What the hell are you looking up at?"

I looked back down at Mr. Bobo. Luke's voice had come from his direction. I looked back up to the sky. "What, you miked the dog? Funny shit, Luke, funny shit. All right, you got me. Joke's over."

Again Luke's voice: "Hey, retard, I'm down here."

His voice was below me. I looked down at Mr. Bobo.

"Why are you finding this so hard to process? You're the one writing the movie with the talking dog."

I was speechless. Mr. Bobo — Luke — sauntered over to the darkest part of the void, his voice moving with him.

"Don't you think that, if you're making a movie about a talking dog, it just *might* be possible that said dog might show up in, oh, I don't know, a dream?" Luke's tiny Chihuahua head stared into the abyss. "That's one big hole. Remember how you said you didn't remember waking up this morning?"

Luke screamed into the hole. "MOTHERFUCKER!"

The hole echoed back: "MOTHERFUCKER! . . . MOTHERFUCKER . . . Motherfucker . . . motherfucker . . ."

I stared at Luke the dog. "Why don't your lips move?"

Luke stormed over — well, as much as a Chihuahua can storm. "And you call yourself a filmmaker? You want the dog's lips to move? You just added three million dollars to the budget. Now the studio is all up your ass. Hey, maybe they want you to direct the thing. Now you gotta deal with the mongoloids at the effects house. You know who I'm talking about — I don't know what it is about playing video games that makes those guys so socially retarded. You want my lips to move?"

Luke the Chihuahua stood front and center. His muzzle twitched.

"Your name is Morgan Beale. You're a writer. Today is your forty-fourth birthday. Your wife is cheating on you. You love somebody else. Somebody else is the only person you have ever loved. You lie all the time. You've never been to see a therapist despite —"

"— that I can't remember the last time I was happy," I interrupted. "I know."

Luke stared up at me. He was talking, but his lips no longer moved. "You want to be happy again? Write. Write something with me. We'll have a laugh. Like the old days."

I did want to write again. I wanted to laugh. I had that same feeling I had when he first asked if I'd like to write with him. I wouldn't admit it back then, but my self-esteem was so low I didn't think I could do anything. I was the person my grandmother was afraid would never amount to anything. Writing that first screenplay, making that first movie, that was the first time in my life that anything good had happened to me. I was almost thirty years old and had experienced nothing but failure. When you walk around with that much self-loathing, failure is the only option.

"Morgan, let's have a laugh." He looked over at the hole. "Push me in."

ZOË

A reporter once asked me if I believed in love at first sight. It was at a Q&A after a festival screening of a movie I had written and directed. It was a love story. A man is haunted by a girl he sees on a train. She is crying. We follow their separate and complicated lives. The couple continually comes within one degree of meeting only to be thwarted at every turn. The film ends as the man dies tragically in an automobile accident. As he stands over his dead body, the girl is standing beside him. The final shot of the film is of the other car involved in the accident. There, dead behind the wheel, slumps the girl.

I first saw Zoë at a bar called the Train Depot, on Main Street in Venice, California. She was crying. I wrote the story line on a napkin. I didn't write the screenplay for another ten years. It was nominated for an Academy Award. When the reporter asked the question, I thought of Zoë. I thought of her brown eyes, her brown hair. I thought of the small scar on her eyebrow. I thought of how her lips pursed before she smiled. I thought of her laugh and how it was sometimes followed by silent clapping, as if she were a ten-year-old girl. I thought of a girl who never had a harsh word to say about anyone. I thought of a girl who cried whenever she saw any kind of pain or injustice. Did I believe in love at first sight? I believed in Zoë.

After that first encounter, I didn't see Zoë again for almost a year. I was a twenty-eight-year-old struggling stand-up comic with dreams of becoming a filmmaker. But who would listen to me tell stories for two hours when I could barely suffer through five minutes in front of a microphone? My self-esteem had yet to catch up with my material. I read most of my jokes from the backs of napkins I'd scribbled on in bars like the Train Depot. I drank alone a lot back then. I was drinking alone a lot lately, too.

A development executive at a successful independent production company lived above me in my apartment complex in Santa Monica. She used to sit with her girlfriends at a table in the courtyard in front of my apartment. They drank vodka, smoked cigarettes, and talked. At first they sccared me. Back then everything terrified me. Especially girls. As I became comfortable with her group I began to read them the jokes I'd written. It seemed easier than letting them know who I really was. Who'd be friends with that guy? I had a talent for constructing jokes, funny story lines, absurd situations. I was quick-witted. If pressed, I couldn't explain where it came from. Pain maybe. When you're miserable as a kid, laughter helps.

I was working as a doorman at a popular comedy club on the Strip — only a stone's throw from the swanky hotel where I learned the secret handshake. The position carried with it several perks: free alcohol and appetizers as well as ten minutes on stage once a week. The girl from my apartment complex was having a drink at a sushi bar half a block from the club. She suggested to her friend, a successful screenwriter, that they catch her neighbor's show. Wasn't he looking for a new writing partner? Wasn't he looking for someone with strengths in comedy? Didn't he need someone to push him into the pit?

Luke liked to laugh. He had one of those rolling, contagious laughs. In the beginning it seemed over the top, but the more I got to know him the more honest I realized it was. That night, I heard his laugh for the first time. We became fast friends. I liked hearing stories about the famous people he knew. I liked hearing about the famous parties he attended. I liked that he had pictures on the walls of his office with famous people posing beside him. He was the first person I knew who had money. He was the first person I knew who didn't bitch when a restaurant check came. He used to put his credit card onto the check while telling a story as if he'd never even consider allowing you to pay.

I began writing with Luke in the summer of my twenty-eighth year. It took us less than two months to write the movie of which strangers remind me every day. I didn't remember much of the process, but I did remember laughing. All the time.

Within two weeks of finishing the script, it was the talk of the town. Everyone knew Luke. Everyone knew Luke's family. But who was this other guy? I went everywhere with Luke. I was invited to every party. The people I met laughed about the script we'd written. They laughed at the way we talked to each other. They laughed at the stories I told, the stories I made up that seemed so real, the absurd situations in which I found myself. About how the scene with the glove happened to me in high school. I began to find some semblance of self-esteem, a comfort zone — albeit not a huge one. I lied about myself. And for the first time in my life, people liked me.

Hollywood never sleeps. There's a party every night. I was having a beer at a bar in Venice Beach called Arthur's. I was meeting Luke there for what he liked to call "a primer." A drink or two before you take on the Hollywood monsters. I was scribbling something on the back of a napkin. When I looked up she was there. Zoë. As if she had just appeared from nowhere. She laughed with her girlfriend. *How happy she looks when she laughs,* I thought. I liked her smile. Gone was the girl who had once been crying. I whispered under my breath, "I love you." I don't know why I said it — it was almost unconscious. No sooner had I whispered it than she smiled. Not a flirtatious smile, but a smile like she felt it, too.

Luke knew Zoë. She had seen us having lunch at a café at the beach and asked about me. Luke brought her to Arthur's to introduce us. When we went for a walk on the beach that night she confided that she had seen me before. At a bar down the street. The Train Depot. She had been crying.

FADE IN:
EXT. FLAGSHIP STARBUCKS — NIGHT

"FADE IN" is where every movie begins. It's the sunrise that brings first light to the story you're going to tell. "EXT." is an abbreviation for "exterior." Screenwriting is all about an economy of words. Like text messaging. Instead of a paragraph explaining the setting, we indicate the setting and leave the rest to the production designer. The production designer, in consort with the director, brings a "look" to the picture. Unfortunately, some kid with computer skills is pushing the production designer out of the picture. That's why every movie you see now looks like a video game. The computer has pushed the architect into the hole.

"OK, we got this big beautiful set that's in desperate need

of the right words," said Luke the dog. "We know where our movie takes place. Now what do we need?"

"We need something to happen."

"Exactly. We need Blanche Dubois arriving on that streetcar named *Desire.* Some guy's hearing voices in his cornfield? Let's build a ballpark."

"George Bailey has lost his way."

"Luca Brazzi sleeps with the fishes."

I smiled. "Luke, I am your father!"

"She's my daughter, she's my sister!"

A pause as he waited for my response.

"Keyser Söze is a sled?"

"All right, funny man, hit the keys."

I saddled up to the typewriter and flexed my fingers before starting to type. Nothing happened.

"What's wrong?" asked Luke.

"I don't know. It's like it's unplugged or something."

I examined the power switch in the rear of the typewriter. It was on. My eyes followed the cord into the Starbucks dispenser. Everything seemed connected, but it wasn't working.

"Maybe it's unplugged inside the machine," Luke offered.

I looked at the dispenser, then at Luke's conveniently tiny Chihuahua body.

"Oh no. I'm not going in there," he said. "Besides, what good would I be? You're the one with opposable thumbs."

Fair enough. I'd have to reach into the cubby and feel for a connection. I rolled up the sleeve on my left arm and reached inside the opening. (God, what a metaphor.) I followed the cord and felt around for the connection. Seemed secure.

"It's plugged in," I said.

Luke jumped onto my chair and then the desk. He pushed his paw onto the keys. Nothing. I continued to fish, turning my body to the typewriter, waiting for any sign of life. When I started pulling my arm out of the machine, a mechanical whir came from inside the green giant. Something grabbed hold of my wrist. *Click.* Something had handcuffed me. I pulled hard.

"Shit, I'm stuck."

"What?"

"My wrist . . . I'm stuck in the machine."

I pulled again, and the typewriter began to write. Luke read along with the racing machine.

EXT. FLAGSHIP STARBUCKS — NIGHT.

I pulled the chair to my side and sat down. I could sit in the chair with little discomfort despite my arm being caught in a vending machine. The keys of the typewriter started flying:

It is the middle of the night,
the staff and customers of Starbucks both a memory and a dream.
In front of the store is a large
Starbucks coffee vending machine,
like a Coke machine but soothing

```
green. The arm of a MAN, 44, is
caught in the opening of the ma-
chine. He waits.
```

"What the fuck?" Luke said. "Waits? Waits for *what?*"

THE MACHINE HAS WRITER'S BLOCK

It seemed like we'd been waiting for an eternity. I was surprisingly comfortable despite my predicament. Every once in a while I reached for the keys of the Selectric to see if there was any response. Maybe I could write myself out of the machine. Every time I touched a key, the same result — nothing.

Lounging on the ground in front of the desk, Luke offered a thought. "Maybe it has writer's block."

"What?"

"The machine, maybe it's having a hard time getting started. You know how it is. Getting started was always the hardest part. 'Fade in' is the ugliest phrase in the English language. You know what the two most beautiful words are?"

I grimaced down at Luke, hoping he wasn't about to quote Dorothy Parker.

"The end," he said, getting up. "Yep, I bet that's what's going on. Writer's block."

It happens to the best of writers. The machine was stuck for an idea. I'd been there. The more you think, the less you get. Luke and I, when we were stuck, would talk about old movies, books we'd read, girls. Sometimes we'd just embrace the silence. That's what the machine had chosen to do. To pass the time, Luke studied the Starbucks, while I stared out at the Hollywood Hills and then back at the big green vending machine. *Big green vending machine.* I laughed to myself. Juvenile, yes, but simple rhymes like that always made me laugh. Doorman Norman from the hotel, and now the big green vending machine.

"What?" Luke said.

"Nothing."

"No, what?"

"It's stupid."

"There's nothing stupid when you're writing. You know that. Some of the things we throw out are bridges to things we use. The machine needs an idea. So what is it?"

"I'm stuck in a big green vending machine. It rhymes."

"That's not stupid. To say that's stupid insults stupidity. Inane is what that is."

"I don't see you coming up with anything to help the machine."

"You mean poetic, like your little rhyme? I'm more of a haiku guy."

"Haiku?"

Luke affected one of those Japanese accents your moron brother-in-law might use when reminiscing about his birthday party at Benihana:

"Haiku: Japanese
syllables of seventeen,
lines: five, seven, five."

"You tell me the definition of a haiku by using it in a haiku? You get that from *Haiku for Dummies?*"

Again with the idiot Mickey-Rooney-as-Mr.-Yunioshi accent: "OK Zen master, try to wrap your mongoloid brain around this Asian beauty:

"Big, dumb idiot
has stuck his hand in machine.
Retard? Yes, retard."

Luke bowed, but it was more of a Chihuahua curtsey.

"That sucked," I said. "And the accent — was Peter Sellers having a sale?"

"You're out of your mind. It was perfectly rendered. Seventeen syllables of pure joy."

My turn. I'd show him seventeen syllables of joy:

"Small, bald, shaking dog
has no balls. This Chihuahua:
white-wine drinker? *Sí.*"

The Spanish word for "yes" served as a tribute to his obvious Hispanic heritage. I leaned down onto the Selectric for my bow. Luke looked down at where his *huevos* should have been.

"I have no balls? Ah, *man* — it's not bad enough they carry me in a sack? And why go with the short-hair Chihuahua? It would have been so hard to make me a long-hair Chihuahua? They wanted Old Yeller, remember?"

My bow had activated something in the machine. Ringing emanated from a speaker above me. The machine seemed to be calling somebody. The phone rang a few more times until we heard a female voice.

"Good evening. Welcome to OnStar."

"Yeah, hi . . ." I said. "I, uhh . . . I'm stuck."

"Yes, sir. I hope that I can assist you. When you say 'stuck,' do you mean broken down?"

"No, I'm . . . stuck in this machine."

"Why do you suppose a machine like this needs OnStar?" Luke wondered.

"Shut up."

"I'm sorry, sir?"

"No, no! — not you."

"Whatever you do, don't use the 'big green vending machine' line," Luke said, skittering around the side of the machine.

The operator's voice was calm and assuring. "So when you say 'stuck,' sir, exactly what do you mean?"

"I put my arm in this vending machine, and it's stuck."

"Sir, is it a Starbucks vending machine?"

"Yes!"

"Sir, let me contact our global positioning satellite and see if we can't get you out. May I put you on hold?"

"Sure."

Elevator music floated out of the speaker: one of those songs you recognized but couldn't name. Tends to happen when you replace electric guitar with synthesized oboe.

"Sir, I'm having a little trouble locating your exact position."

Luke returned from behind the machine. "Ask her why the machine needs OnStar."

I kicked at him.

"HEY!" he screamed. "Watch where that foot goes! I'm dealing with a totally different piece of machinery here."

"So am I."

"Sir, is somebody stuck there with you?"

"Not exactly."

"HEY!" Luke screamed up at the speaker. "Why do you have OnStar on THE BIG GREEN VENDING MACHINE?"

The operator chuckled. "Big green vending machine . . . Oh, there you are! Oh, my. You're quite a ways away. Let me just . . . well, that's not good. Sir, I'm going to have to send a technician out to your location. May I have your name, last name first?"

"Beale. B-E-A-L-E, first name Morgan."

She punched a few computer keys. "Ah, we have you in our system."

Wasn't that the truth, I thought.

"So you're not having any trouble with the Jeep or the Porsche?" she continued.

"No."

"It's just you and the machine?"

"That's right."

"Oops, I just unlocked the Jeep. Is it somewhere safe?"

"It's in my garage."

"Oh good."

I didn't have the heart to tell her I didn't know where my garage was anymore. She clacked away at the computer keys.

"Mr. Beale?"

"I'm here."

"Sir, our technician is on his way. Is there anything else I can help you with this evening? Dinner reservations? Information on a show?"

"Ask her why the machine has OnStar!" Luke persisted.

I stared him down, so Luke screamed up at the speaker. "HEY! WHY DOES THE STARBUCKS MACHINE HAVE ONSTAR?"

"Who cares?" I stage whispered.

"I care." He pouted.

"It's a stupid question."

"There are no stupid questions at OnStar," the operator chimed in.

The cheerful voice vindicated Luke. "Thank you," he said haughtily to the speaker.

"To answer your question — and of course I would like to preface my answer by saying that we are still in the early phase of the program — it seems that Starbucks customers like to get a beverage and then, as they leave, find out where the next closest Starbucks is. Knowing another Starbucks is just around the corner provides great comfort. Also, studies show that some customers who drink an enormous amount of Starbucks products find it difficult to think for themselves. OnStar and Starbucks have teamed up to guide wary travelers across this great big Starbucks nation of ours. Is there anything else, sir?"

Luke looked up at the speaker. "Yeah, you give information on shows?"

"We do indeed, sir."

"Why was *Cats* such a big hit?"

I wanted to launch his tiny Chihuahua ass into the hole.

"Oh, my. I think a better question is why such a glorious Broadway show ever closed in the first place. I'll always have great memories of Sir Andrew Lloyd Webber's inspirational book and music."

"She liked *Cats,*" Luke mumbled to me. "What's that say about the 'big green vending machine' line? She chuckled, remember?"

"Do you have any idea how long the technician will be?" I said to the speaker.

"Well, let me see, sir. Hal, what's your twenty?"

Over the speaker came a new voice. It didn't sound very inspiring.

"Ah . . . well . . . it's, uh, foggy. Just headin' out now. Got kind of a late start 'cause I locked the keys in the van. Had to wait for my buddy to bring me a coat hanger from his apartment. Shouldn't be long."

"Sir, did you hear that? Hal had a bit of a problem getting started, but it shouldn't be long now."

"Thank you," I said.

"Thank *you*, Mr. Beale! You have a good day, and thank you for choosing OnStar, a subsidiary of Starbucks!"

The only thing less inspiring than Hal's voice was his story. But hey, I was the idiot with his arm in a machine, so what did I know.

"He locked the keys in the van?" Luke laughed. "The OnStar technician — no, scratch that: Hal the OnStar technician locked his own keys in the van? Someone call Alanis Morrissette. We just found her some actual irony. This is shaping into one hell of a picture. Exterior, hole, Hal's OnStar van approaches. Mistaking the gas for the brake pedal, OnStar Hal loses control of the company vehicle, plowing into dog, man, and machine. Fade out."

RELEASE THE CHIMPS

Hal might have sounded a bit dim, but his timing was spot on. No sooner had we hung up with the OnStar operator than we saw the headlights of Hal's van. The light climbed straight up the inside edge of the hole, poking into the sky like those searchlights you see in a World War II documentary or at a movie premier.

Problem was this van's headlights were so dim there was no chance they'd alert any superheroes or spot enemy combatants. The grill of the van reared up into the air, the chassis half out of the pit. Righting itself, the van maneuvered like a tank coming out of a trench. Hal guided his vehicle into the lot in front of the Starbucks.

Hal rolled down his window — no doubt to avoid any further mishaps with his keys. He climbed out in his crisp white OnStar coveralls with "Hal" embroidered on the chest. He carried a bright, shiny metallic toolbox. He was stocky, with a shaved head. He pulled an OnStar baseball cap from his back pocket and slapped it on his pate. He looked like a milkman who likes to lift weights. Hal smiled as he approached the machine. Wow! Look at all those teeth. Now he looked more like a beaver who likes to lift weights.

"You Mr. Beale?"

"Yeah."

"Who the hell else would you be?" Luke volleyed. "Oh my God! What's with his teeth? Hide all the wood!"

Hal didn't get very far. As he made his way toward me, the grandeur of the flagship Starbucks stopped him cold, drawing him like a hypnotist's pocket watch. He was enchanted. Mesmerized. Spellbound.

Luke studied Hal, who now resembled a statue. "Uh-oh. Looks like Big Hal has set his sights on our store's maple woodwork. Probably gonna build himself a dam near the hole. Invite all his beaver friends over for a cookout."

Hal was reading the musings on the walls, his lips moving with each word. After each epigram, he nodded slowly and muttered to himself, "That's so true. Starbucks wisdom is so true."

Luke watched Hal in disbelief as he read to himself. "Would you look at that? Beaver's lips are moving." Then Luke let fly one of his seventeen-syllable gems:

"Big dumb-ass: lips race,
reproducing seed intact.
His balls remain. Why?"

Had Hal heard it? He continued to read. Was the allure of the Starbucks wall so hypnotic that Hal could focus only on it? Or was I the only one who could hear Luke?

"Wow, they have TVs inside!" Hal exclaimed. "Wow, five of 'em! You can watch TV while you wait for your drink. The guy who runs Starbucks is going to be president some day."

Hal pulled a shiny new cell phone from inside his crisp white coveralls. He flipped it open and took pictures of the Starbucks with his camera phone. "The guys in my band are never gonna believe this."

Hal held his phone out for me to see the pictures he'd just shot. He scrolled through picture after picture: the TVs, the musing wall, the bright shiny home of the barista. Then he felt a twinge of anxiety. "You don't know when they're opening, do you? I mean, is there, like, a grand opening or something? Is there a list? Do you know if there's a list?"

"I don't know," I said. "I just got here."

Hal gazed longingly at the store. "I hear when they first open a store they give away all kinds of stuff: hats, T-shirts, macchiatos, caramels, chocolate. And for that whole day you can keep coming back. They never say no. Do you know if they're hiring?"

"I don't know. Like I said, I —"

Then the lightning bolt Hal was searching for.

"I'm gonna shoot some video!" He held the phone up for me to see. "You can shoot ninety minutes of video with this phone. T-Mobile. They're one of the companies that teams with Starbucks to make our coffee-and-wireless experience a happy one!"

"Morgan?"

Luke was peering into the shallow end of the hole. It was hard to see at first. Then I caught a glimmer. It was some sort of cable that climbed out of the deep end, ran the length of the shallow end, and snaked up the ramp. The metallic cord crossed the ground to a grappling hook that had hooked onto the back bumper of OnStar Hal's van. The cord snapped and pulled taut.

"Something wants out," Luke said nervously.

And that's how it happens. The idea. You think you're stuck, but all you need is a man in white coveralls with a video camera. You have a setting and you want to tell a story. The story of your world, his world. The world of the man in the coveralls. The world of the man in the hole. If you tell the story of the man in the hole, you can save him.

A beam of light appeared. Not the dim beam of some company van, this was a bright light, a powerful beam reaching into the sky. A hand was now gripping the cable. Another hand over the first. Climbing into view was the light source: a flashlight strapped to a hardhat. Then a face.

I knew this face.

Michael Chapman was fifty-one years old. He taught American lit at a small New Hampshire college. He was average height with soft white features. You might say he was bookish. He wore his hair short due to his conservative Southern upbringing. He married his high-school sweetheart, Angela. They had two children: a boy, Sam, and a girl, Evy. He had written four books. He began with a detective novel, graduated to a thriller, and found his voice with farce. His fourth book takes place at an estate in the Hamptons. It's called *The Chihuahua in the Blue Prada Bag.* For forty-five weeks he was the darling of the *New York Times.* Since then, he took a sabbatical from teaching and relocated to Los Angeles. He lived in a rented craftsman bungalow just below the Hollywood Hills. He was making the rounds at all the Hollywood parties and premiers. Michael Chapman had been photographed in all the right restaurants. His new "girlfriend" was one of the last five contestants on a reality show that took place on an island. In the pictures, Michael Chapman looked like he enjoyed "celebrity."

But what a difference a day made. The look on Michael Chapman's face here was nothing like in the pictures. This was a man on the brink. He mustered all his strength to pull himself into the shallow end of the hole, fighting to catch his breath. He rolled over on his back as if this were the end of an exhaustive prison break. His hardhat lay on the ground beside him. His hair shot out in several directions. Only a straitjacket could complement this look.

He lay on the ground for a moment, then sat up quickly when he saw me. He donned the hardhat as he pulled himself to his feet. He glanced at Hal and his video phone. Hal was still trying to decide on a proper angle, oblivious to the writer. Chapman crossed through the shallow end like a soldier on recon. He ducked his head, climbed up the ramp, and ran toward the van, lurking against its side so as not to be detected. Michael Chapman stared at me, then looked quickly away. He recognized me. He had panic written all over his face.

"Please don't tell them. I know you're with them, but you're a writer, too. We're not like them. I know you understand, just . . . I'll give you everything if you don't tell them."

"Them?"

Michael Chapman looked from side to side. He came over and leaned in close to whisper the secret. "You know, the movie people. Promise you won't tell."

"Tell what?"

He looked at me as if I was the crazy one. "That I want out."

"Of what?"

"The hole."

Ah, yes.

Luke hummed the theme to *The Twilight Zone.* "Submitted for your approval: one Michael Chapman, a writer with conscience. He took to fame and fortune like a cheap crack whore. His groveling has garnered him a permanent place — in the Twilight Zone."

Chapman looked at Hal, who was still looking for the best shot. He held his thumbs in the shape of a frame, looking like one of those pretentious wanna-be filmmakers.

"Is he with them?" Chapman asked.

"Him? God, no. He's with OnStar."

Chapman's eyes grew wide. "OnStar? The map people? The people who unlock doors? The people who get you home?"

Chapman gazed at Hal with the same longing you see in

the eyes of people at church on a Friday afternoon, those "I've lost all hope" eyes. Those "where's the miracle?" eyes. "Do you think he would take me home?" The former New Hampshire professor looked back at the hole. It visibly terrified him. "I don't want to go back. I just want to go home. I miss my wife. I miss my kids. I liked being average."

Chapman began to cry. "Will you ask him to take me home?"

Before I could even open my mouth, a faint rumble sounded from inside the hole. A horrified Michael Chapman turned to the dark pit.

"Oh God . . . please, no!"

The noise grew louder and louder. It sounded like the spinning blades of a helicopter. Wind began to swirl all around. With a thundering roar, a rotor came into view, then the black body of a chopper, big as a gunship. Michael Chapman ran back to the safety of the OnStar van, pinning himself against its side. The helicopter now hovered above the Starbucks. Chapman reached up ever so slowly and turned off the flashlight on his hardhat. Then he took the hat from his head and cautiously set it on the ground. He stood motionless. Michael Chapman was pretending to be invisible.

A beam of light shot down from the helicopter, engulfing him.

"MICHAEL CHAPMAN. YOU ARE IN VIOLATION OF THE CONTRACT. PLEASE RETURN TO THE HOLE."

Chapman mouthed frantically for help. Whatever he was saying I couldn't hear. What I could hear sounded like skidding tires. It was faint, but so was every sound beneath the pounding blades. Then a car jumped out of the void. Like the big black death wagon, this vehicle also defied gravity, leaping over the ramp and landed squarely in front of Chapman. It was a black Lincoln Town Car, its headlights fixed on the shaking writer. Again the voice from above.

"MICHAEL CHAPMAN. YOU ARE IN VIOLATION OF THE CONTRACT. RETURN TO THE HOLE."

Chapman stared helplessly into the headlights of the Town Car. There was nowhere to go. Or was there? Suddenly he turned and ran, screaming, "NO! I CAN'T GO BACK! LEAVE ME ALONE! I CAN'T! I JUST WANT TO GO HOME!"

The light of the helicopter followed. Where was Michael Chapman running? The spotlight stayed on him, like in one of those freeway chases where the suspect suddenly leaps from the car and tries to outrun the cops. Then Chapman stopped cold. Actually, something stopped him cold. Michael Chapman had hit the wall. What he thought went on forever was just a cleverly painted backdrop. Welcome to the movies. His crumpled body lay just below the HOLLYWOOD sign.

The speaker from above called out to the Town Car. "RELEASE THE CHIMPS!"

The doors of the Town Car flew open. Four enormous chimpanzees raced out. They were wearing dark blue and gray business suits. Good cuts: the kind you see agents, producers, and studio executives wear. The chimps ran for Chapman, who was cowering at the edge of the sound stage. They picked him up and hoisted him above their heads as if performing some kind of jungle island ritual: the natives marching the young virgin writer toward the volcano. When they reached the edge of the hole, they looked up to the chopper as one, waiting for orders.

From the speaker: "IS THERE ANYTHING YOU'D LIKE TO SAY?"

Chapman fought back tears. "I could'a been somebody. I could'a been a contender."

The speaker responded: "YOU DID NOT WRITE THAT. YOU NOW HAVE AN UNORIGINAL THOUGHT PROCESS. INTO THE HOLE."

And just like that, the chimps tossed the bookish professor from New Hampshire into the the hole. The helicopter dipped into position, its light searching the burial site of the former writer. The nose of the chopper turned back to the chimps, and the voice spoke again. "MISSION ACCOMPLISHED. SECURE THE PERIMETER."

The helicopter descended into the void, the roar of the blades quickly fading. The four suited chimps sauntered back to the Town Car. Wait — one stopped short. He walked over to the OnStar van and reached down for the hardhat Michael Chapman had been wearing. He turned the headlamp on and shined it around the perimeter. All clear. The four chimps climbed into the car and closed the doors. The vehicle backed up, pulled down the ramp, and dropped into the hole.

"Were they wearing Armani?" Luke said.

"I think so."

"They should weave that into some sort of ad campaign. 'We can even make a monkey look good.' "

Something moved under Hal's OnStar van. It was Hal, his crisp white coveralls no longer crisp and no longer white.

"The floor of this sound stage is filthy," Luke observed.

Hal climbed out from underneath the van, terrified. Four primates and a helicopter had completely sullied what had been, up to now, a genuine Starbucks moment. His hands were shaking. He looked down at his video phone. "S-somebody needs to see this."

Hal held the phone up for me to see, but I was too far away. He closed the phone and started walking away.

"Where you going?" Luke asked.

"The man they threw into the hole. People need to see this. He's like that guy who just wanted us all to get along. I, I have to show this to somebody. It's wrong."

Hal climbed into his van. The engine turned over, and he threw it in reverse, tires skidding backward. He peeled out of the Starbucks lot and raced for the ramp, swerving until he gained control. The van disappeared into the dark of the cavity.

OnStar Hal was gone.

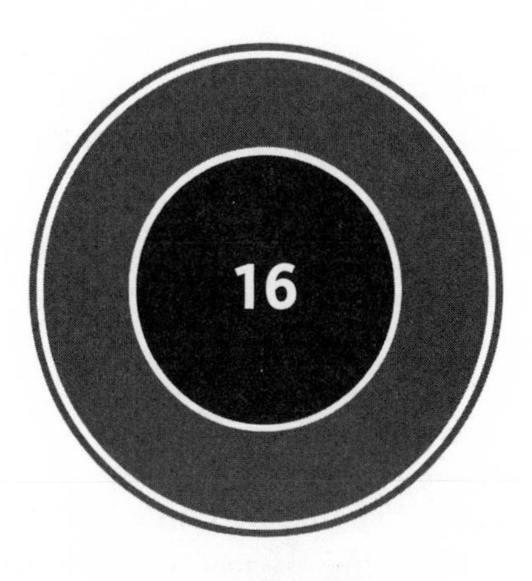

I HEARD HER SMILE

Luke lay on his stomach, staring at the stars around the HOLLYWOOD sign. We were waiting for the next scene to begin.

"What was the name of that boat you had?"

I'd forgotten about my boat. It was so long ago.

"*Zoë's Rose Tattoo.*"

"That's it — *Zoë's Rose Tattoo.* Wasn't that the name of Zoë's band, too?"

"Yeah."

"God, that boat was fun. Remember that little black bikini Zoë used to wear when we'd go to Catalina?"

"What are you trying to say?"

"That Zoë had an ass that looked like it was carved by Rodin."

I looked down at Luke.

"What, I got no balls, so now I gotta quit thinking like a man?"

Thinking about Zoë made me sad.

"What a voice she had," Luke continued. "A rock-hard ass and a rock-and-roll voice. Man, she was hot. You ever talk to her?"

"Not really."

Zoë sang in a band that had a dedicated underground following. We made the perfect modern-art couple: the screenwriter and the punk-rock-hippie chick. If Luke had taught me how to be cool, Zoë taught me how to feel. Before Zoë, I didn't know how. Whenever I felt even the slightest twinge of happiness, I thought something bad would happen. Whenever I smiled, I heard my grandmother's voice in my head: "Nobody likes people who are too happy. Happy people are gloating. Happy people are naive to the real world. Ignorance is bliss. Happy people are ignorant people."

Zoë wasn't ignorant. Luke wasn't ignorant. I didn't want to hear that voice anymore. I wanted to hear Zoë's voice. I wanted the only voice in my head to sing, "I love you." Zoë used to sing to me as I fell asleep. Her voice made me smile. I used to fight falling asleep because I was afraid that when I woke up her voice would be gone, replaced by that voice in my head I was trying so hard to forget.

Zoë used to say that the one thing she wanted to teach me was how to cry. The good kind of crying, the kind you associate with joy. I cried like this only once in the twenty-six years since my eighteenth birthday. I had bought a thirty-six-foot motor yacht for fifteen hundred dollars. It gave me something to do while Luke was in preproduction on the movie of which I was reminded daily.

I worked on the boat from morning to sunset every day. I cleaned the hull. I took it completely down to the wood, years of neglect peeled away. I restored the cabin to its original teak. After months of failure, I finally had the twin engines running. Zoë was there every step of the way. It seemed only right to name the boat for her.

At sunset we ate and drank as we watched the sailboats return from sea. It was the first time in my life I could truly say to myself that I was happy. I shared this with Zoë as we watched the sun setting. Her smile was so big that I heard it.

She leapt to her feet. "We need to celebrate!"

She swung over the railing and jumped onto the dock, reaching for the ropes that fastened the boat to the cleats.

"What are you doing?"

"Let's take her out! Let's go watch the sunset on the ocean!"

"But . . ."

I was terrified. I didn't want to look bad. That was why I lied so much. I wanted people to think I'd done the right thing, the cool thing, the funny thing, when actually I hadn't done anything at all. I was afraid. I didn't want to fail, so I never tried. But there was something in Zoë's smile that was safe. So I told the truth.

"I don't know how to drive a boat."

"Do you know how to pilot one? Cars you drive. You pilot boats."

I loved when Zoë made fun of me. Here I was, the writer, the guy with the dictionary, and she knew so much more than me.

"Morgan, the first time she goes out it should just be us."

"She?"

"The boat. You know, you're lucky you're cute, because I don't know that you're going to get anywhere with your smarts."

I laughed. "OK, let's take her out!"

She laughed and clapped — like she always did when she was excited — and raced around the dock untying cleat after cleat. I went to the bridge and stared at the wheel, frozen. Zoë leapt onto the deck and threw her arms around me from behind. It was like Christmas for her. She spun me around and kissed me.

"Come on, cap'n! Let's get her out on the high seas! If you're lucky, I'll let you put on a pirate hat and have your way with me."

I turned the ignition. "You are a very strange girl."

"Arrrrrrr!"

The first engine turned over, then the second.

"Now remember, ease her out," she said. "Check your rearview. Hands at ten and two on the wheel. We don't want to end up on *Red Asphalt.* Do they have boating accidents in *Red Asphalt?*"

I eased the boat out of the slip. Zoë stood aft and used her feet to stop us from hitting anything. As I turned the boat into the harbor, she ran back to the bridge and leaned the weight of her body against mine, making me feel safe.

I brought the boat to a stop just outside the mouth of the harbor, facing the setting sun. Zoë took my hand.

"I love you." She smiled as she said it.

My eyes filled. It was the first time anyone had ever looked into my eyes and said those words.

POLISH THE TURD

Luke was bored. You could hardly blame him. Not much excitement since OnStar Hal followed the chimps into the hole. I couldn't think of Zoë anymore. It was too painful. There was only one thing to do. Wait.

When Luke and I wrote together, we created countless ways to pass the time when we were stuck for an idea. When you're waiting for that next big idea to crawl out of the hole, you fall back on the same things you did while waiting for the next idea to hit paper. It's really the same thing. You're waiting for something that doesn't exist — yet. So how do you kill the time in between? You can snack, but if you're going through a particularly dry patch, you are in danger of becoming a fat man on a crowded elevator. In our current predicament, my arm was blocking the only avenue for sustenance. You can drink coffee, toss playing cards into a hat, smoke, drink. Alcohol presents its own set of problems, as Luke reminisced.

"After writing and drinking all day, I hopped a red-eye to Vegas, where I checked into the MGM Hotel with a suitcase containing thirty-two pairs of underwear, one tube sock, a jar of Vaseline, and a pair of bib overalls. I spilled my suitcase at the lobby elevator and spent the next four hours being stalked by a man with a banjo. Lesson? Never write or pack drunk."

Luke looked inside the hole.

"Anything?" I asked.

"Nope."

"You want to play Polish the Turd?"

"Nobody to polish."

"OnStar Hal?"

"Too easy."

"Michael Chapman?"

"Too sad."

"The chimps?"

"Too weird."

In the old days, when we were stuck, procrastinating, or both, we would go to a bar, a coffee shop, or a mall and play a game called Polish the Turd. You pick out a mark and fill in the blanks. You give them lives they couldn't possibly achieve on their own. How could they? They were turds. Color their past with so many checkers that they could play the game of life at breakneck speed. What did they do for a living? What did they score on the SATs? Were they married? What did the tattoos on those discreet parts of their bodies say? Most writers call this back story, the part of your characters' lives that will never find paper.

"Want to play Big Dick?" I said.

"Big Dick" is a slang term in dice for "ten." Your opponent names a subject. It could be cheese, subatomic particles, Japanese emperors, whatever. You then have to list ten instances of that subject in alphabetical order. The idea is you pick a path and don't think. It's a good game for a writer. You have ten seconds to name the ten examples. The score from each round is added to the previous round, and you play to a hundred.

"Yeah, I'll play," Luke said. "Who goes first?"

"Or we could play Rock, Paper, Scissors, but I'm a pretty sharp guy, and by the looks of those mitts you're pretty much always going to come up paper."

"Funny stuff from the guy whose second sheet is stuck in a pop hole."

"I'll go first, and I'll make it easy on ya. All you need to do is remember your last visit to the park. Breeds of dogs. Ten, nine . . ."

Luke fired back. "Akita, beagle, Chihuahua, Dachshund — both smooth and wirehair . . ."

"That only counts as one. Six . . ."

"Fox terrier, Gordon terrier, Jack Russell, Lhasa Apso, pug, and Schnauzer."

"Nice."

Luke sat confidently. "I toyed with putting my ex-wife in there, but I wasn't sure how the judges would score it."

"You rolled a Big Dick. If your wife were here, she'd be on all fours."

Luke got up and shook out his hind legs. "I'm thinking of updating my résumé. Do you think it's pretentious for me to list my past lives? You gotta admit, pharaoh of Egypt looks pretty good under job skills."

"You gonna list that stint at the Donut King, too?" I knew what he was doing. He mentioned Egypt, caught me leaning, and then went a whole different —

"Superheroes! Ten, nine . . ."

"Aquaman, Batman, Captain America, Captain Marvel, the Flash, Green Lantern, Incredible Hulk, Robin —"

"No side kicks. Five . . ."

"Spider-Man, Superman . . . ahh, shit!"

Luke sounded the buzzer. "You got nothin' but a tiny dick."

Then, grease in the fire: "Wonder Woman? Xena, Warrior Princess?"

"Xena? You're like half a fag. Can I get you a white-wine spritzer?"

It's amazing the crap you retain when you're a writer. Luke taught me that everything matters. Good stories are in the details. I forgot how much I liked the game. I suffered through writing now. It was never like that before. Before, I wrote about what mattered to me. I tried to make a statement by veiling my worldview with humor. Michael Chapman did the same. I was guilty of jumping into the hole, too. Or maybe Hunter pulled me in. In the end it didn't matter. Either way I was in the dark.

Luke prepared for my well-crafted, military strike. Where

would it come from? Hindu gods, Greek gods, Roman gods? Old Testament figures, varieties of beer? Could it be organized crime families or notable pirates? Luke was shaking.

"Are you nervous?"

"The shaking? Just part of the package."

"Not all of which you have, my furry friend."

"I'm the only one who's rolled a Big Dick here," he noted.

I smiled, then launched my offensive. "Pornographic magazines! Ten . . ."

In one easy breath, Luke rolled: "*Barely Legal, D Cup, Entertainment Weekly, Hustler, Jugs, People* magazine, *Playboy, Swank, Us Weekly.*"

I furrowed my brow. "I'll have to go to the judges, but first I'd like a clarification. When you say *Playboy,* are you pushing the dirty articles or the tasteful photographs?"

"The photographs."

I nodded approvingly. "Rock solid. Although there was some talk of disallowing several items, since equating celebrity magazines with porn insults pornography."

Luke laughed but quashed it halfway through and counterattacked. "Imaginary places! Ten . . ."

"Whoa, whoa! Clarify."

"Imaginary places from literature, folklore, songs. Good enough?"

"Commence with the count."

"Ten . . ."

"Atlantis, Camelot — both Arthur and Kennedy, but not the actor Arthur Kennedy —"

"Still only one. Seven . . ."

"Emerald City, Gilligan's Island, Gondor, Gormenghast, Lilliput, Metropolis, Shangri La . . ." I looked up at the flagship Starbucks. "This place."

"More specific. Three."

"Starbucks."

"That really exists."

"Does it? OK, the Twilight Zone. Big Dick."

"You went small in the first round. This is my game, baby. You can't take me."

"Yeah? Time to kick you where it hurts. Slang terms for condoms! Ten . . ."

"Brutal! Cockbag, jimmy hat, love glove, raincoat, rubber . . ."

"Seven, six . . ."

"Sperm cozy, spunk nict, the Catholic middle finger —"

"'The' is the definite article. Catholic precedes cockbag. Proceed. Three . . ."

"Taco warmer, vaginator —"

"Time. The last two are suspect. In the judge's opinion, both are euphemisms for penis."

"Taco warmer? It's a female condom."

"You just made that up."

"It's called the FC. Look it up. And what, a female can't wear a condom? Pig."

"Fine. Explain vaginator."

"I'll use it in a sentence: Mild-mannered Marvin Rooney was the laughing stock of the mall refuse detail. Little did they know that at night he fought crime hidden behind a cowl made of latex condoms. How differently they would treat him if only they knew he was — the Vaginator."

"That's retarded. Even if I give it to you, we're knotted at twenty-nine."

"Fair enough."

We had settled comfortably into a routine when there was a huge explosion in the hole, followed by what sounded like a rocket launching. The initial blast was so loud that I almost wrenched my confined arm out of its socket. We both shielded our heads and recited a litany of choice Germanic words.

Racing into the sky was an enormous blue van, a blazing lightning bolt on its side. The van arched like a missile, fire shooting out of its twin tailpipes. Suddenly the rockets shut down, and the van stopped in midair. With a loud *pop,* an enormous parachute inflated above the van, which floated gently to the ground. It was like a great blue alien craft had landed in some cornfield or faraway desert. On top of the van perched an enormous satellite antenna. Was this where the death ray would come from? On the side of the van was printed EYEWITNESS NEWS TEAM. Yes, this was where the death ray would come from.

All the doors flew open at once. Seven people streamed out, like a SWAT team mobilizing at a hostage standoff. Each member of the Eyewitness News Team performed an appointed task. One man carried lights. A woman set up a makeup table. Another man dragged cable toward a street light, then shimmied up the pole. Here came a woman with a clipboard, flanked by a man with a television camera. A man in shorts carried a tripod. They all maneuvered around the hole. The woman with the clipboard barked orders.

"We'll set up here. Hole frame left. Put Brock's mark here."

Shorts dropped to his hands and knees. He chalked separate spots for the tripod and Brock, then opened the tripod as the cameraman mounted the camera on the stand.

Clipboard called, "See if you can get the HOLLYWOOD sign in the same shot as the hole."

Cameraman looked through the viewfinder and gave a big thumbs up. Then the angels began to sing on high. From the van came a man with skin so golden brown, teeth so pearly white, and hair so perfectly placed that Narcissus himself would have called for pizza to be delivered to the makeup chair. Golden Brown once devoured an entire pizza served to him on his vanity mirror. Then, after a horrible bout of self-loathing, he stuck his toothbrush down his throat so as not to gain back any of that college ten he'd worked so feverishly to remove.

The production came alive. Golden Brown went to makeup as glorious light illuminated the hole. The satellite dish atop the van began to turn, first right, then left, the great dish searching for that elusive signal. Finally it stopped, pointing directly into the hole. A technician leaned out of the back of the van and shouted, "We've made contact!"

The woman with the clipboard was the segment producer. A segment producer can be male or female. The one thing they all have in common, males and females alike, is a penis. Sometimes, like hyenas, the women have bigger penises than the men. That's the only way to get the position.

The segment producer also doubles as director. This particular segment producer is typical of most: ill-fitting clothes, aggressive, self-assured. Think ten pounds of shit in a five-pound bag. She was hangin' out all over the place, still shaking her ass like an eighteen-year-old transvestite. Likeable? Not really. If she was lucky, she might eventually become a chimp in a Lincoln Town Car. Were Luke and I witnessing a miracle? Were we beholding the early stages of a media event?

Shorts crossed to his mark.

Luke thumped his tiny Chihuahua tail. "Big Dick, where do we stand?"

"Round three. We're knotted at twenty-nine," I replied.

Luke's mind was racing. The segment producer nodded — the light now adequate.

"What do you say we put Big Dick on the back burner?" Luke said.

"Spot a turd?"

"Yeah. Shorts."

GET A GRIP

It had been a long time since I had played Polish the Turd, which isn't really a game because there's never really a winner. You're just in it for a laugh. You fill in the blanks until the mark possesses a life less ordinary.

"I'll give you first crack," Luke offered. Luke always liked to give me the first shot. It gave him time to get creative. Even though first crack is the less enviable position, I agreed.

"Born Kevin Mackey. Sarasota, Florida. He's twenty-eight years old. Drinks Coors Light. His first memorable sexual experience involved a plastic Fanta bottle. While fantasizing about his big sister's best friend, Lolly, his penis became so engorged that the plastic vagina got stuck around the base. He heard his mother pull into the drive, and he panicked.

The harder he pulled, the harder Lolly Fanta pulled back. Then, mustering all imagination, and with total disregard for life or limb — that is, what little limb there was — little Kevin Mackey used a pair of his mother's pruning shears to relieve himself of Lolly Fanta."

"Pruning shears?"

"He was assaulting Lolly Fanta atop mommy's potting bench."

Luke nodded approvingly. "Touché." Luke took a tiny breath and then his turn.

"Kevbo has a panther tattooed above his left nipple. Every morning he grits his teeth after their thorough brushing, flexes his chest, and growls. As you've established, little Kevin enjoys masturbation. You could say it has become an addiction. When he masturbates, Kevbo thinks of the lead singer from a very prominent eighties hair band. Behind the singer's zipper of gold is a vagina — a mangina, if you will."

"That sounds so clinical."

"Would you have preferred I said 'mussy'?"

I laughed one of those unconscious laughs I'd lost so many years before. It wasn't always what Luke said but how he said it. Kevin Mackey reached inside the van's sliding doors and pulled a television monitor into view. My turn.

"A full fifteen years after the incident on the potting bench, Kevin Mackey was playing a drinking game with the other security guards at the water park where he'd found a summer job. After a twelver of liquid courage, he lowered his shorts to the floor and revealed a scar near the mangled foreskin of his uncircumcised penis. The scar bore a remarkable resemblance to the initial that graces Superman's chest. Kevin Mackey used the demonstration to explain why he had chosen the name Kal-El, son of Jor-El, for his Lolly Fanta fucker."

Luke laughed as Kevbo ran cables from the television monitor he'd set up next to Brock's mark.

"You think he's married?" I asked.

"Nah, he's quirky, like his first sexual experience. A happy Friday night for him involves a mop handle, a goat, and an old eight-by-ten of Nancy Reagan. When he does find himself with a girl, let's just say he can't quite satisfy her needs. This, of course, is due to an innate selfish quality in his lovemaking, which he established those many years ago when he soiled his little Lolly. . . . He has been known to wear the ribbed condom inside out. He likes the way it pinches."

Kevin Mackey ran a new cable from the television monitor to the camera and tripod. He fumbled as he poked the head of the cable into a camera port, fighting to find the connection. "A simple male-to-female connection," Luke remarked. "If he can't find a hole when there's this much light, can you imagine him in bed?"

The cable finally found its home. Kevin Mackey ran a hand through his hair, an arm across his face. Now he was sweat-free. He thrust his hand into his shorts, shifted Kal-El, son of Jor-El, to the left, and withdrew a pack of cigarettes. He'd earned it; he did just poke the camera.

Kevin Mackey was what we in the industry call a grip. A grip is a production mule. Heavy lifting? Get a grip. I normally liked grips; they always had alcohol in their trucks. On a production this small, a grip usually had to multitask. That was why they'd allowed Kevbo to deal with something as dangerous as his own brain. He rolled up the sleeves on his Pendleton shirt. There on both forearms Kevbo had tattooed flames — the kind of flames he should have painted on his Camaro.

"Flames?" Luke barked. "The retard has *flames* on his arms? Life isn't moving fast enough for him? I'm done with this guy. Ain't no amount of creativity can help his character. If we're lucky, he'll fall into the hole."

NOW REPORTING, RANDY SAMPLES

The cameraman climbed behind the camera, put his eye to the viewfinder, and flipped a switch. The television monitor flickered to life, the image of the hole on the left and the HOLLYWOOD sign behind. The image grew and shrank until the cameraman found an acceptable frame. He waved Kevbo onto Brock's mark and then crossed in front of the camera with a light meter. Good news — plenty of light outside the hole.

"We're ready to roll," the cameraman said to the segment producer.

And again angels began to sing on high. Brock climbed out of the makeup chair, the great tan god. He smiled and nodded approvingly at the makeup girl. What a wonderful job she'd done. She smiled sheepishly. What an honor it had been to work on cheek bones so sharp, on skin so flawless, on a chin with such a perfect cleft. As he turned into the light, it was hard not to notice that his teeth were so white they looked blue. Had the cameraman taken the blue light into account? How could he, with Flame Boy as the Brock proxy? Kevbo's teeth resembled butterscotch pudding. Had Kevbo been snacking in the van?

Brock was that reporter the network always had its eye on. When a big story broke, the phones rang. "Is tan Brock on site?" "Send Brock and the pearly blues." All the big stories went to Brock. Global warming. The war on terror. Gay marriage. Bird flu. Janet Jackson's star-studded tit. If there was a category-five hurricane, Brock and cleft were battling the storm in a rain poncho.

Tan Brock walked in slow motion, his torso dipping into his enormous stride, his arms swinging high as he lumbered along. His mother had probably once remarked, "Somebody this good-looking should slow down a step so the ne'er-do-wells of the planet might behold God's greatness." Slow-motion Brock replaced Kevbo and his flames. Good news for both: Tan Brock would soon be on display to the world and Kevbo could scoot back into obscurity.

This new character was a welcome sight for my Chihuahua friend. He was quivering with delight. "Ahh . . . Finally a character we can work with! What say we hit the burners and start cookin' this turd with gas?"

"I defer to your tiny brain, O Great Brown One."

"I'm about to drop a brown one on your foot."

Luke stretched out his tiny front paws and tried to crack his knuckles. No go.

"What's with the stretching?" I said. "It's not a prizefight."

"It was thirty-two years ago this June that the Immortals of the Sun squatted from the sky and squeezed out this perfectly browned biscuit of joy."

"He's the face that launched a thousand shits?" I interrupted.

Not a hitch from Luke. I'd forgotten what a formidable opponent he was.

"Brock Robinson is the most senior reporter for one of the giant networks. These days his eyes lie squarely on the anchor position, which carries with it the clout that Brock Robinson so desperately craves. Seems he's got a bit of an inferiority complex. Imagine Napoleon if he were six-foot-four. You see, his beginnings are humble. Long before the bon vivant, before there was even a glimmer in the eye of this man about town, there was a gawky ten-year-old in Mundfordville, Kentucky.

"Born Randall Samplested, he was known to parents Alma and Randall Sr. simply as 'Randy.' However, because of an overactive mucous membrane, due in part to his daily battle with hay fever, Randy was known to classmates and townsfolk alike by a different name. Randy liked to pick his nose, and on more than one occasion a newfound chewy treat found its way onto the soft red cushion of Randy's tongue. The town suggested several monikers. The local grocer, one of the world's first Trekkies, offered 'the Mucanoid.' 'Randy the Miner' carried the dual connotations of Randy's junior status as well as nose mining. To be expected from the man who read not only the local paper but the big paper from Lexington as well. The playground bully called him Snot Monkey. The town finally came together as one, and the boy became known thereafter as Randy Samples. He carried this nickname with him until the day after his high-school graduation, when he climbed aboard Greyhound number ninety-seven for Big City, America. His first stop was Atlanta, Georgia, home to Teddy CNN."

Quite a picture Luke was painting. No gray areas. I felt like I was really beginning to understand Brock Robinson. As for Randy Samples? I felt ashamed at the lack of creativity I mustered when naming Kevin Mackey. And my Fanta bottle? Luke might have been dead for thirteen years, but he was obviously still writing.

"Like to take the reins?" he offered.

"I am awed by your greatness."

"It is time to use the Force, O mighty warrior," said my tiny brown Jedi Master. Brock Robinson was looking over the copy he would soon share with the world, nuggets of gold that would roll off his tongue, which hadn't tasted snot in over two decades. The makeup artist was trying to touch up perfection. Who did she think she was? I went for it.

"By age twenty-one, Randall Samplested stood six feet, four inches tall. He lived in a three-story walk-up just above a Chinese laundry run by his landlord, Mr. Fu. Mr. Fu had taken an awkward liking to young ward Samplested. Every morning Mr. Fu called to the growing giant, 'I tink you glo' one mol' inch big, Landy! Evly day, one inch mol'!'

"Then, one morning, Randall Samplested's life changed forever. Having just received his associate's degree from the local Georgia Peach Junior College, the former Randy Samples was searching the want ads. His red marker found an ad from local news affiliate WATL:

"'Do you have a high-school diploma? An associate's degree?'

"Randy Samples answered aloud, 'I have both.'

"'Would you like a career in television?' Randy Samples thought, *TV, yeah . . . That'd show everybody back home.*

"The ad continued, 'We are seeking self-motivated people with strong communication skills. Please send résumé to . . .'

"Randy could hardly believe his luck. He ran down the stairs of his three-story walk-up, on his way to the library, thinking, *What's a résumé?*

"As he passed the doors of Mr. Fu's laundry, he heard the old man call, 'Whe' the file, big Landy? . . . I tink you glo' anothel inch, big Landy! Soon you be big as whore brock!'

"*Yes,* thought Randy Samples. *I'm gonna be on TV, and soon I'll be bigger than the whore brock.*

"And that's when it hit him. *If I'm going to be on TV, I'll need to change my name. Everyone on TV changes their names.* Every time he watches prime-time entertainment shows or late-night talk shows, he is always awed by the stories of those who began to court fame with the simple yet humbling experience of pretending to be somebody else. Who would want to see Randall Samplested on TV? Worse yet, Randy Samples. *I'm not that little kid who picks his nose anymore,* Randy thought to himself. *I'm bigger than this whore brock.*

"'Brock,' he said aloud. 'BROCK. Like "rock" with a B.' He dared not tempt fate. He had 'Brock,' but the transformation was incomplete. He couldn't possibly be Brock Samplested. That would only be half-pretending. He heard Mr. Fu's magical voice, 'Whore Brock.' What whores did he know? There was that *Pretty Woman* whore — the smiley one with horse teeth. What was her name? He remembered that movie he saw on TV where the young college graduate sleeps with the mother of the girl he will soon fall in love with. He identified with the lead character's sense of loneliness, especially when he looked into his fish tank or swam in his pool. TV Brock would have a fish tank. TV Brock would have a pool. What was the college guy's name? He knows the mother's name: Mrs. Robinson. He knows because he says it over and over as he pleasures himself on the weekends. Only on weekends. More than that would be dirty. Would it be dirty to use Robinson? Brock Robinson? Man, that sounds good. 'Rock' with a B, and then Robinson. He promises God that he'll never pleasure himself again if he can just use Robinson. Of course he pleasured himself again, but the transformation was already complete.

"Brock Robinson did in fact learn what a résumé was. He was in fact hired by local affiliate WATL. His stardom came quick under the watchful eye of an aggressive young segment producer. He only had to blow her for a year. That's how Randy Samples became the self-motivated, strong communicator known to all as Brock Robinson, glorious television reporter."

"So we agree that Brock Robinson is dumber than a bucket of shit?" Luke asked.

"That's why he was attracted to the news media. The skill level is easily mastered. The right name, the right tan, the right teeth. He's a no-brainer."

"News reporters are like real-estate agents with —"

Before Luke could make his point, Brock Robinson looked up from his copy and said to the segment producer, "I'm good to go."

The mood on the set shifted. The segment producer went to her cell phone. "Brock's good to go." She nodded, then shouted, "Go to the feed!"

The van came alive. Headsets appeared on the segment producer and other notables. The television monitor took on a beautiful, soft-blue color, across which waved a red emblem that read EYEWITNESS NEWS TEAM SPECIAL REPORT. The soft-blue screen gave way to the confident, paternal face of the anchor.

"Good evening." His voice was deep and composed. "I'm David Hume, and this is an Eyewitness News Team Special Report. Last night we reported the story of a former writer who was assaulted by four chimpanzees and thrown into a hole."

Video filled the frame of the television monitor. There it was, OnStar Hal's shaky footage of the four chimps racing from the Lincoln Town Car. Michael Chapman's screams of terror pierced through the noise of the helicopter. The chimps marched the terrified writer to the hole. The video jerked up to the helicopter and back to the chimps. Then the voice from the helicopter that gave the order: "INTO

THE HOLE." Michael Chapman was gone. David Hume reappeared and turned to face another camera. This was important stuff. The segment producer pointed to Brock and began the countdown on her fingers. "We're live in five, four, three . . ."

"With more on this breaking story, we go now to Eyewitness News Team Reporter Brock Robinson, who comes to us live from the site of this tragedy. Brock?"

Full-frame was Adonis incarnate, Brock Robinson, no smile.

"Thank you, David. I am standing at the very spot where this horrific crime was indeed committed. At approximately three A.M., the victim, writer Michael Chapman, tried to climb out of this hole."

Brock pointed to the hole, then walked us through what we'd just seen on video. The camera followed obediently.

"The chimps in question drove out of this hole in a black Lincoln Town Car. They chased the victim to the edge of the sound stage. Then they carried Mr. Chapman back here to the edge of the pit, where the helicopter ordered them to throw him. Here, into *this* hole."

Luke and I made eye contact. Brock Robinson was indeed dumber than a bucket of shit. On the monitor was a split screen: David Hume in studio and Brock Robinson on site.

"Brock, what do we know of the chimp assailants?"

"Yes, David. After airing the video on last night's newscast, Eyewitness News received several hundred tips, which were turned over to the authorities. This led to the arrest of the four assailants. They have been identified as Benjamin

Levy, president and CEO of the Creative Artists Agency; John Jacob Malden, president of Paramount Pictures; and producers Dawn Ford and Brad Berman. The voice from the helicopter has yet to be identified."

"Brock, does anyone know if terrorism played a role?"

"There is some speculation that there may be a Middle Eastern link, since superagent Ben Levy and producer Brad Berman are Jewish. And Paramount president John Jacob Malden just last week gave the green light to the bin Laden biopic *The Twenty-Seventh Child.* As for producer Dawn Ford — she has a reputation for being the only chimp in Hollywood who can identify the Middle East on a map."

David Hume nodded approvingly at such crackerjack reporting. "I see. Brock, have you found any sign of racism with regards to this crime?"

"David, the four chimps, as well as writer Michael Chapman, are white. However, there is a black character who appears in Mr. Chapman's book, who on more than one occasion utters the N-word."

"Do you think there's any kind of link there?"

"I certainly wouldn't rule it out."

"Has anyone spoken to God?"

"Indeed I did, David. He assures me that everything will work out in the end."

"Well, that certainly is reassuring. Brock, how do you see this all playing out?"

"David, I think it's still too early to tell. But what I can tell you is that a horrible crime was committed here. Rescue crews from FEMA have yet to arrive with the equipment necessary to probe the hole for the missing writer. But I can assure you that Eyewitness News will remain on site until Michael Chapman is pulled from the dark of this very dark hole." Brock looked deep into the lens. "Reporting from the hole, this is Brock Robinson, Eyewitness News."

The segment producer acknowledged a voice in her headset. "And we're out."

Lights dimmed. A collective sigh of relief. The cameraman nodded at Brock.

"You hit it outta the park, bro'."

The segment producer praised the stellar performance. "Great piece, Brock," she said, scratching her balls.

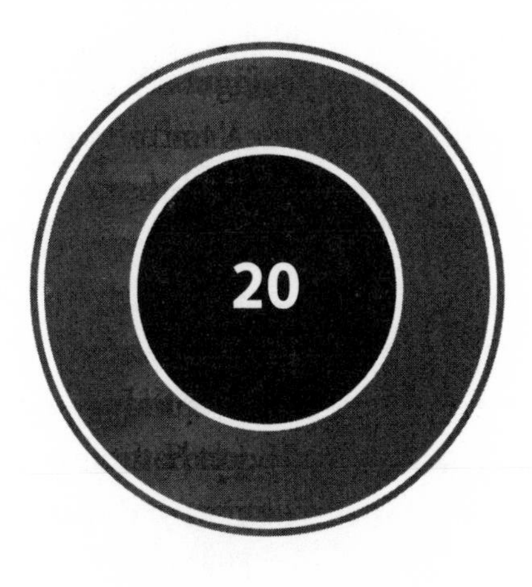

OPTION THREE

The Eyewitness News Team was smoking and talking around the mother ship — well, not all of them. The segment producer and Kevin Mackey had gone around behind the flagship Starbucks to see if they could break in. A little-known fact about people in entertainment and media: when on site, they believe that rules and laws no longer apply. Breaking and entering? *We're here to report a news story!*

I began to wonder if this group was actually qualified to do its job. Here I was, a guy sitting at a desk with his arm stuck in a machine, and nobody had even thought of coming over to ask me if I saw anything. They were reporting on a story about some guy who was thrown into a hole. I had the perfect vantage point, but nobody from Team Eyewitness seemed to give a shit. I felt like I was in high school again: nobody noticed me in high school.

Inside the Starbucks, the segment producer and Kevin Mackey were walking past the warm raspberry walls. She yelled something into her headset, and the group around the van scrambled. Two team members climbed into the van and reemerged with two folding tables, which they set up next to the van. The cameraman and his assistant approached the front door of the store, which the segment producer unlocked from inside. The hands that set up the tables were soon inside the store. Various grips climbed behind counters and disappeared into the supply room. The group emerged from the store toting box after box of supplies to the folding tables next to their spacecraft. Luke was weaving through their legs as they worked. Nobody noticed him either. Were we invisible? Luke made his way back to the vending machine.

"What are they doing?" Luke asked.

"Setting up a craft service table. Team Eyewitness is setting up camp."

The craft service table is ground zero for snacks. It's the area where people of "craft" gather for a shot in the arm. You've been throwing a framing hammer all day so that boutique in the next scene will look magical, and now you're a little low on juice. The answer is the craft service table. Get a Coke and a muffin. You're making a movie, reporting the news. You need to nibble on something other than your inflated sense of self-importance. At the end of the day, you throw out what you don't eat, then talk about circulating a petition for Feed the Children. Need an analogy? You've been working hard on that sales presentation since lunch. Your performance is slipping — you leapt headlong off your Zone Diet with that baked potato. Take the team to Starbucks. Starbucks is the average Joe's craft service table. Go on, have the antidote! Four shots of espresso with nonfat-milk foam — that'll help you create that perfect bumper-sticker slogan to combat childhood obesity!

Luke scrutinized the looting news team. "So where do you think we are? With the script, I mean."

"Well, the machine has been doing relatively little writing of late. I think the hole is the real writer."

"Yeah?"

"Yeah. If you look at the hole's script . . . I don't know . . . My guess is we're at the beginning of the second act. We've got a hole, a missing writer, four chimps in custody, and the beginnings of a media circus."

"That's one weird hole," Luke mused. "Old-school, you know?"

Old-school was right. The hole was setting something up. Which isn't how movies are made today. The new school has an idea and fashions a script. You don't need acts, just a gimmick you can sell in the TV spot. Fact is, you don't need a story at all. Movies have been so bad for so long that nobody even expects a story anymore. If they get one, it's a bonus. What they do expect is some cool scenes strung together in an *attempt* to tell a story. First get the idea on paper in the form of a script. Have six guys "fix" it, and then hire as many famous, beautiful people as you can. Teach them some martial arts and insert a few pretty-people fuck scenes, and — presto! — you're done. Who doesn't like to watch really good-looking people pretend to fuck?

Then, about halfway through, you have a few options.

You can chop the pretty people up. In this scenario, the movie ends with the hottest chick and the hottest dude killing whoever has been killing the other pretty people.

Option two is that the pretty people become special. They become superheroes, superspies, or pretty people with superskills. These movies usually end with the superevil guy and his secret lair blown up by the nuclear device the superspies have somehow thwarted seconds earlier. In this option, when two of the superpretty people fuck, something usually catches fire. That's what happens when superpeople's genitalia connect.

The third and rarest option is to say something original.

The hole had chosen option three.

AMERICA BACKS OUT OF THE HOLE

The Eyewitness News Team devoured the contraband confiscated from within the walls of the flagship Starbucks. Luke and I agreed that — because of the group's blatant disregard for the sanctity of a place that millions consider their house of worship — the gloves were off. Turds needed polishing, starting with the gang's ring leader.

"There's a lot to be said for a man's name," Luke said. "Can you imagine if bin Laden's name was JoJo?"

"JoJo bin Laden?" He was buying time.

"He wouldn't have made it through the first Al-Qaeda mixer. The second people saw his name tag, they would have laughed him out of the tent." His eyes narrowed. "What if Hitler's mom had called him Buddy?"

"Quit stalling."

"'Buddy' definitely doesn't carry the same weight as 'Adolf.' Buddy Hitler makes cold calls for the phone company. 'Hello, my name is Buddy Hitler. Are you happy with your current long-distance provider?'"

The segment producer powered her way through a turkey and swiss on five-grain with accompanying fruit-and-cheese plate. Luke went after her.

"Brenda Jo Gunderson — or 'Mile High' to her classmates at Carver High School in Oberlin, Kansas. The nickname is not a fond memory for Brenda Jo, as its beginnings can be traced to a nefarious episode that occurred as the Carver High marching band made the long trek from the plains of the lower Midwest to the great centennial state of Colorado.

"Band Jam Nineteen-ninety was all anyone could talk about the summer before Brenda Jo's senior year. Why else would Brenda's grandfather Neal pay seventy-five dollars to have dinner with the morning DJ from 'All Country, All the Time' KLCN? Her family heartily supported her dream of one day taking her tuba and dotting the 'i' at her grandfather's alma mater, Ohio State. She owed it to Poppy to make this band jam a memorable one.

"What Brenda Jo didn't know was that the only event she would remember from this trip — of which she was reminded every day of her entire senior year — would occur after blacking out from drinking three cans of Hamms Light Summer Lager. How could this happen, you ask? Hammie Light was Poppy's favorite beer. She thought she'd given the hand job in the bus to graduate-student-teacher Reed Holliwell. 'What do you mean it was the bus driver? He was Mexican. Reed has red hair!' Turns out bus captain Hector Cervantes likes to nap in a red knit cap from his favorite football club in Zacatecas, Mexico. When Hector finished the final leg of the trip, he smiled, donned his favorite piece of headwear, and winked at Mile High Gunderson."

My mind was rolling. How could I top that? "Mile High Gunderson?"

"When I started with Brenda Jo, I toyed with a BJ, but that seemed a little on the head, you know? So I countered with Mile High and the BJ became a hand job."

"Nice touch."

"Details, baby, details. Grab a bat. You're up."

"It was years before Brenda Jo Gunderson could make a fist and move it north and south. To this day, she will only purchase cars with automatic transmission. When you open the glove compartment of her new six-cylinder Volvo three hundred, a very different name appears on the documentation inside. Mile High Gunderson is no more. Just as she replaced her brass instrument with the safety-tested Swedish import, Brenda Jo was replaced by the golden-blond streaks of Missy Wright. That's Miss Wright to subordinates. Brenda Jo was a community-college dropout who looked like a package that had been kicked around by UPS. Missy Wright is a forty-four D cup. Her plastic surgeon says it's the best work he's ever done. Missy Wright has been nipped, tucked, gathered, pleated, quilled, and fluted. Missy Wright has been 'jobbed' by the best 'hands' money can buy."

"Extra credit for the air quotes, due to your obvious handicap," Luke said. "Top-notch wordplay, too. Tell me, does Missy Wright have any tattoos?"

"Yes. On the inside of her right wrist, Missy has the Chinese symbol for 'peace.' This way, when she gives herself a hand job, she is reminded that she is finally at peace with her past."

"BJ Wright has a tendency to steal, so we'll label her an antagonist."

"Who do you want to polish next — the camera guy?"

Before Luke could answer, the hole spoke: two long blasts from what sounded like the horn of a semi, then the roar of a diesel engine, followed by grinding gears. Whoever's driving isn't that smooth with a stick. The gears engaged and triggered that incessant, mind-crushing BEEP-BEEP-BEEP heard on every reversing truck and van these days. The hole was ready to get back behind the keyboard. The second act was about to begin. Luke and I waited patiently. The Eyewitness News Team also turned their less-than-capable journalistic eyes to the hole.

The red taillights of an enormous semi appeared. The big rig rolled onto the ramp and started to ascend. As Team Eyewitness got an eyeful of the truck, they feverishly cleaned up their tables. Kevin Mackey dashed to the van. If they didn't move quickly, the monster was going crash their little party. Grips scrambled to clear a path for the trucking giant just as the semi extended fully out of the hole and rolled onto the lot in front of the Starbucks. The light from the news setup caught the side of the trailer, illuminating four gargantuan smiling faces and one giant robot head.

I knew these faces. I knew that robot. My wife was friends with these faces. My wife was friends with that robot. My wife woke up every morning with these faces. My wife woke up every morning with that robot. It was a trailer for America's favorite morning show. It was a trailer for *Good Day, America.*

Good Day, America set the standard for morning magazine shows — that perfect smattering of news, weather, and celebrity, peppered with all-important fashion, makeup, and cooking tips. They were the original Starbucks: smiling faces to share your morning cup of coffee with.

Good Day, America has been copied by virtually every other network morning show. The smiles of the perky hostess and handsome host anchor the show. The funny weather guy is a little overweight. If he's a minority? Well, now you're cookin'. The serious one sits at a news desk. This could be a woman or a man, but a serious pretty woman with great fashion sense is ideal, as she may be called on at any moment to step in for the perky hostess or handsome host. It's good if she lets her guard down once in a while, too. It tells America that we shouldn't take the world so seriously. Yes, war is bad, but is it so unpleasant when you wrap it up in an Hermès scarf?

A MIDDLE FINGER DOWN THE THROAT OF THE HOLE

Act two began with a bang. People piled out of the hole. First came the production team for *Good Day, America.* There must have been sixty technicians and crew in the first wave alone. A production of this magnitude took an army to bring it to life. Oddly, though, it wasn't just crew climbing out of the hole. There were fans, too. The loyal fan base of *Good Day, America* had come to see its favorite personalities in person.

"The hole must have eaten some bad food at a Fourth of July picnic, because what's climbing out resembles a white-trash parade," Luke said.

The sound stage was becoming a full-blown production. The network had decided to broadcast from the hole. The network had decided to make Michael Chapman's story and the subsequent arrest of the chimps the number-one story in America. Brock Robinson was still on point. He would do live remotes from the hole. The flagship Starbucks was alive and well, and it was the perfect set for *Good Day, America.* The televisions inside were humming with celebrity news and weather. The news crawl indicated that the terror alert was elevated. Orange is such a warm and inviting color.

They had set up two couches where Perky, Handsome, and Round Minority Weather Guy would sit. Any celebrities dropping by to say "hi" or to promote their latest projects had a place on the couch as well. If we were lucky, there would be celebrity baby news this morning. The world stops when two of the pretty people are having a baby together. Would they interview the doctor who caught fire taking the bun from the oven?

Barricades lined the front of the flagship Starbucks. The gathering fans needed caging. No telling how some of them might react at the sight of someone who was actually on TV. The giddy group of onlookers stared at the empty couches, waiting with great anticipation for Perky, Handsome, Serious Girl, and Round Minority Weather Guy.

The Eyewitness News van had been moved from beside the hole to beside the *Good Day, America* truck at the far end of the sound stage. No one seemed to care about the hole — or the man in the hole, for that matter. *Famous people are coming!*

More people streamed out of the hole. At least a hundred fifty fans were staring at the empty couches. Technicians scurried to set up television monitors outside so that the fans out front could watch the show as it would be seen by the rest of America. Producers had realized that people were more comfortable watching the show on TV. Some people wouldn't even watch the monitors. They'd watch the show on the four-inch screens of their camcorders as they recorded the show on the monitors in front of the show.

More technicians were working behind the safety of Starbucks glass. They readied the *Good Day, America* set: perfectly matched pillows for the couches, knickknacks around the aquarium behind Handsome's seat. They secured rows of lights overhead. Three cameramen worked out the logistics of running cables across the polished floor. Everyone moved smoothly. This crew had been together for a long time. This was a family. The craft service table was the size of a small country — like Monaco without the roulette wheels. Every treat imaginable was piled high. An army does march on its stomach, and this glorious TV army was about to assault the dark of the hole. America needed to know. America would not forget the man in the hole. America would rally once again. The chimps were gonna pay. Why? We didn't know why. We had to wait for the media to tell us why. Soon we would know.

Luke and I watched the madness unfold. The monitor next to the hole took up the *Good Day, America* feed. The crowd roared as Perky, Handsome, Serious Girl, and Round Minority Weather Guy stepped on set. Like Brock Robinson, they, too, walked in slow motion, like astronauts boarding a shuttle. Perfect hair, perfect teeth. Look at those smiles!

Handsome's suit was perfectly tailored. Look at the legs on Perky! Had RMWG lost some weight? He looked great! Serious Girl was such a fashion-forward hottie.

The loudest applause came for the one entity that would never dare move in slow motion. That would be against all that is holy in this great Starbucks Nation of ours. You see, the morning landscape was extremely competitive. In order to keep its toehold in that essential number-one spot, the powers at Network Central had introduced a gimmick so captivating that *Good Day, America* shot a full ten points above its nearest competitor.

Bob Botty was the most recognized robot in the world. Well, since the president who got us into that war with Iraq. You know the one. Generous Electric spared no expense in developing this metal Will Rogers — what the TV critic over at *People* called him. Other critics likened him to a good-looking Winston Churchill, called him HAL with pizzazz. Bob Botty received over two hundred requests for marriage *daily.* His blog received a hundred thousand hits a day. His was the most downloaded image on the Internet — including porn. He had written nine books on topics ranging from makeup and dating tips to China's burgeoning economy. Everyone wanted to know Bob Botty.

He wasn't much to look at, really. He was, in fact, a retired bomb-squad robot. His mechanical arms, it turned out, were very good with the cooking demonstrations that had long served as the cornerstone of the *Good Day, America* program. That was how he began. Next came makeup applications and fashion tips. His movie reviews were top-notch. He was also a terrific poker player, as you might imagine. And he wasn't just limited to Texas Hold 'Em. He'd been programmed to run the gamut.

Movie stars, TV stars, rock stars — every celebrity that graced the set of *Good Day, America* had signed Bob Botty's metallic body. My wife signed Bob Botty. There was so much ink on his chassis that, if he were human, Starbucks would have fast-tracked him to shift manager.

Brock Robinson slowed onto the scene. Segment Producer Missy Wright appeared. The cameraman took the camera off the tripod and hoisted it onto his shoulder. Kevin Mackey held the cabling like it was the train of a wedding dress. They were going to shoot the next story down and dirty. Maybe Brock was thinking of going into the hole himself. After all, that kind of reporting won Peabodies.

As Brock stared down at his copy, the monitors sounded the *Good Day, America* anthem, a familiar, comforting piece that made people smile. A bright shiny cartoon sun rose high above caricatures of the four anchors. Then Bob Botty rolled through, lassoing the four anchors and dragging them across a map of America. Cue laughter as they climbed into their cartoon set.

"And we're on in five, four, three . . ."

Lights up. Applause. The music faded, and we were live from Starbucks and the hole.

The crowd shook with silent excitement as their morning demagogues exchanged pleasantries. Bob Botty teased our favorite weatherman. Not so fast — our round friend had the perfect response! The crowd laughed.

What nuggets of wisdom will they teach us today? What's in style this morning? Will you teach us how to make a perfect mojito? Mmmm, I love ceviche! You're serving it in an avocado? What genius thought of that? Hey, we're going to help single mothers who are pregnant find suitable mates. A fashion show for women with osteoporosis? I hope you're thinking of decorating that hump with sequins! The Jesus Diet? You mean I just look at my meal and ask, "Would Jesus eat this?" Did Jesus like chili?

That's the formula: small talk, a few jokes, what we'll learn today — but first the news. Serious Girl adopted a serious tone. She held her copy in her hands but never looked down. Had she memorized the story? No, she was just reading the teleprompter. Maybe that was why they chose her to be Serious Girl. Brock could read . . . sort of. Not only did Brock's lips move when he read to himself, they also moved when somebody read to him.

There it was again on the monitor: the chimps at the hole, Michael Chapman high above their heads, the shot of the helicopter, the command from the unidentified voice, then the chimps tossing the innocent man into the hole. Serious Girl became increasingly serious. This was going to be the story of the year. A collective gasp arose from the audience. *That's why we're here? Why didn't somebody tell us sooner?*

Brock Robinson stood dead center, his chiseled features bathed in light. He walked us through the crime again, not one word or one step changed from the story he told before. He did point more, and with great emphasis. It was like one of those Axis propaganda films. Mussolini, Hitler, Hirohito — they all pointed with great emphasis. How would Brock Robinson look in a military uniform? How would he look addressing the troops? In a way, he *was* addressing the troops. He was their military leader. Brock Robinson was the leader of Starbucks Nation.

Brock finished his remote. Perky, Handsome, and RMWG were mortified. *How could this happen? Is anyone safe?* They wanted to know more.

Perky launched the first question. "Is the hole near any schools?"

"Yes, there are at least fourteen schools within twelve miles of the hole. A day-care center is fifteen miles from the hole," Brock confided.

"Fifteen miles?" She was too terrified to take it any further.

Handsome weighed in with studied gravitas. "Has anyone checked to see how many registered sex offenders are near the hole?"

"There are more than seven thousand registered sex offenders in the county, and no doubt a number of them have probably had their eye on the hole," Brock reported.

Handsome followed up his hard-hitting question with another. "There have been unconfirmed reports that an inland valley gang has been operating a meth lab inside the hole. Can you confirm this?"

"I'll sniff around and see if I can collaborate the story."

Luke and I went to the judges. He meant corroborate.

"I read on the Internet that by the end of the day more than a hundred thousand people could fall into the hole," RMWG added.

Handsome and Perky nodded. They'd read the same thing.

"Well, in my experience, if you read it on the Internet, you can't take it lightly," Brock said.

Wait, Handsome had a suggestion. "Would it help to put a warning label next to the hole?"

Brock nodded. Why didn't he think of that? If he was ever going to make anchor, he was going to have to start thinking outside the box. After Handsome's suggestion the questions really started flying.

"Could this be an avenue for bird flu?" — "How will it affect global warming?" — "Gay marriage?" — "Stem cell research?" — "The sex trade?" — "Do you think the hole will affect gas prices?" — "Is there oil in the hole?" — "Could North Korea fire a nuclear missile from inside the hole?" — "Has anyone asked Tom Cruise about the hole?" — "How about the Middle East?" — "Could Al-Qaeda get in through the hole?" — "Worse yet, could *Mexicans* get in through the hole?" — "Should we call the Minutemen?"

It was a great day for news.

Brock suggested we all say a prayer for the hole, a prayer that God would relieve us of the hole, a prayer for all those around the hole. *Good Day, America* went to commercial.

The lights went down; the monitors went dark. The fans turned their attention to their cell phones, iPods, and PDAs. Nobody made eye contact or talked with anyone else around them. They talked into or took pictures with their phones. Thumbs bobbed as ecstatic fans alerted their wireless playmates that they'd just seen Bob Botty *live!*

Several production assistants emerged with free coffee. A mad scramble ensued as hundreds of hands reached for lattes, cappuccinos, and macchiatos. Behold the considerable multitasking skills of Starbucks Nation: one set of hands on their Starbucks treats, the other on their wireless binkies. Starbucks Nation was at peace.

"These people are crazy," Luke said. "Nobody even cares about the guy in the hole. I mean, they saw the chimps toss him, but all they asked about was the thing he was thrown into. And what's with the people behind the barricades?"

"They're only here to see somebody famous."

"It's depressing."

"You can't really blame them."

"Yes, you can. They're watching the crap, aren't they?"

He had a point.

"I'm starting to understand the hole," he continued. "What goes in is culture. What comes out —" he indicated the fans and the set of *Good Day, America* — "is *that.*"

FEMA IS A FOUR-LETTER WORD

Perky and Handsome introduced the hottest young Internet film critic: a twenty-six-year-old overweight college dropout famous for sneaking into advance screenings of movies. You really had to impress him before he gave his supersize meal of approval. His Web site received more than 175,000 hits a week. That class at the Cerritos Junior College of Film and Television — coupled with his stint as floor manager for the food court at Universal Studios — gave him a unique perspective. The support of his loving mother and father were invaluable, as was the inspiration that he was meant to share his thoughts and impressions with the world.

When invited to critique the hole, he asked, "Who's in it?" Then he joked that the only thing in the hole was a writer.

"Nobody cares about writers," he said. "Writers are nobodies, and, if nobody is in the hole, it must not be very good."

I hate critics. Those who can, do. Those who can't, teach. Those who can't teach get into automotive sales, real estate, retail, or fast food. Those who can't handle sales or service critique those who do, those who teach, those who sell, and those who serve. Critics don't create anything anymore. By definition, a critic is always looking for something wrong. Why is the guy who used to tell us the movie times now telling us what he thinks? The guy who won the contest to be the weatherman at the local TV station is now telling us what's a "no-no" and what's a "go-go"? Critics have always been wrong. Or maybe Van Gogh really did suck. The world *is* flat, Columbus. Hey, Galileo, you're an idiot! Critics will always say, "I'm right." Why? Because they hate you for going after your dream while they stayed behind. And why are they so mean? — as if the idea of presenting your art offends the zeitgeist of mediocrity. Criticism used to be an art form, like art itself. Now it's just a mean kid with a blog. Critics hover only one step above the paparazzi.

Brock was set to do another feed for the late sleepers who were just tuning in to *Good Day, America.* Missy Wright and the cameraman discussed a new angle for the story so as not to bore those who had already beheld the hard-nosed investigative piece.

The lights on the set came back up. Thumbs sent final texts and ended calls. Earbuds popped out of ears and coiled around iPods. All eyes turned to the monitors. The network was promoting one of its own shows. Where better to do it than on morning television's number-one program?

The network's hottest magazine show, *24/24,* was doing another episode on Internet predators called "Holding the Hands of Our Sexually Curious Children." David Houston earned his fame by parading these predators on TV. He posed on the Internet as a thirteen-year-old girl or boy with a profile on MyFriends. The profile featured a picture of a blossoming young girl or boy wearing a "Hot 'n' Naughty" T-shirt — pink for girls and blue for boys. When Mr. Predator showed up at the agreed location, reporter Houston and his camera crew ambushed him. Houston broadcast the footage of Mr. Predator for all the world to see, concluding each program by showing the world pictures of the predator's parents, grandparents, siblings, children, and friends. They knew the sicko, so why should they escape?

Church groups and all majorities with "moral" in their title claimed Houston as their hero. His grass roots organization, Scarlet Letter, swelled to half a million members. This week's program coincided with a visit to Capitol Hill, where he and a senator from Georgia introduced legislation whereby a sexual predator would have the word "PERVERT" tattooed on the shaft of his penis. They gave this sound explanation: "If you are in a public restroom known to be frequented by sexual predators and you are staring down at the penis of a man next to you, you are safe if you see nothing more than pee. If you see 'PERV' or 'PERVERT,' you are in a danger zone. Terror level elevated. You should immediately contact the office of the senator from Georgia with a detailed description of the predator. If you could provide the senator with an address, too, that would really be helpful, as it would expedite the entire process."

Good Day, America had derailed our game of Polish the Turd. We couldn't make up the reality these idiots were living. We stared into the hole. The movie it was writing was a tragedy. *Please, hole, send us something to laugh about. That's why we're here, isn't it?*

The hole heard our prayers. There came from inside — was it a bell ringing? The melody grew louder, and then we saw it. Trundling out of the hole was a FEMA truck labeled with bright red letters. It wasn't very inspiring. Actually, it looked like an ice-cream truck. The music we'd heard turned out to be "The Entertainer" by Scott Joplin.

Circling around, the FEMA truck made a sharp left away from the fans and the set. On the monitor, you could see the truck clear as day as it passed behind Brock. It stopped fifteen feet from the hole — or tried to stop. The truck's screeching brakes proved less than responsive; it continued to roll toward the void. The driver pumped the brakes as hard as he could, but he was quickly losing real estate. The FEMA truck finally stopped as the front two wheels fell over the edge of the hole, spinning silently. The driver poked his head out the window and wiped his relieved brow.

The driver's door opened. Out came the lone representative of the top-notch government agency. Nobody had alerted FEMA to the tragedy until now. Our government official had been enjoying his half-caf latte at the Starbucks cart inside the Capitol rotunda when he learned of the disaster. Thank God for illegal immigrant Manny Hernandez and his video phone.

"Looks like we need to go to commercial," said Handsome. "In the meantime, Brock, can you get an exclusive with the FEMA representative?"

Brock smiled his winning smile and approached Mr. FEMA. "What do you say?"

"Sure — if you can get me an autographed *Good Day, America* mug." Mr. FEMA laughed. "I'd also *love* to meet Bob Botty."

Then Perky chimed in. "Brock, ask the FEMA guy if he'd like to participate in the cooking demonstration. We're making gumbo!"

"Good idea," chirped RMWG. "It'll probably be a disaster!"

Everyone laughed. They had completely forgotten about the writer in the hole.

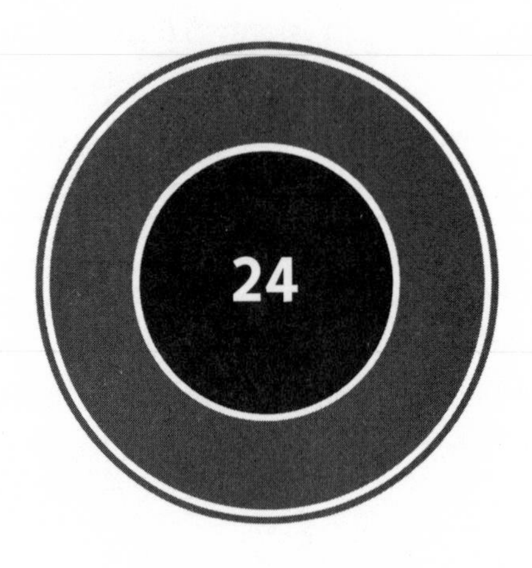

DISASTER, RELIEF, DISASTER

There was work to be done before Mr. FEMA could speak to the morning team. Luckily, the producers at *Good Day, America* realized that the work he was about to do was of the utmost importance. They agreed to help him in any way they could. Mr. FEMA enlisted the help of a few grips from the show. Eyewitness News grip Kevin Mackey lent a helping hand, too. Was it safe to take the terror alert to a softer color? Pale blue, maybe? The grips positioned three ladders tepee style, with a pulley at the top and a crank made from a cable spool.

"What do you think it is?" I asked.

"I think they're trying to build a winch," Luke said.

Mr. FEMA pulled miner's coveralls over his government-issue golf shirt and khaki pants.

"Oh my God." Luke laughed. "They're gonna lower this idiot into the hole!"

Mr. FEMA secured a miner's helmet to his noggin. The grips fitted a harness over his shoulders.

"All right," said Luke, "we've fallen way behind watching this train wreck. We don't have much time before they drop this moron into the hole. Here's what I propose: Polish the Turd, lightning round. Perky, Handsome, Weather Guy, and the serious girl with the twenty-five-thousand-dollar engagement ring who just did the report on the famine in Africa — they all need names."

The whoresome foursome were making baked Alaska. What happened to the gumbo?

"Fair enough," I said.

"Serious Girl's real name is Gretchen Braut," Luke began. "She had a nasty case of scoliosis and had such low self-esteem in high school that she actually said yes to Clark Mooney when he asked her to prom. Full-Moon Clark tipped the scales at three hundred pounds. After they made several turns on the dance floor, English teacher Mrs. Beckerschmidt commented loudly to Principal Marshall that the happy couple actually spelled out the word 'SO.'" Luke paused. "Want a crack at Weather Guy?"

"Sure. Big guy's handle is Charlie Arden. He's had one homosexual experience in his life. It was with his wife, Candice. A little role-playing game of search and seizure got out of hand. While dressed as a prison guard, wife Candice performed a cavity search with a flashlight. They spent three hours in the emergency room searching for two D batteries. They have six-year-old twins named Jake and Josh. Jake once asked his mommy why Daddy becomes so agitated whenever the lights go out."

"Six-year-olds don't use words like 'agitated,'" Luke said.

"They do when their dad does weather on a nationally syndicated morning show."

"Hmm. I'll allow it."

Luke turned his polishing rag to turds Perky and Handsome. Perky playfully pushed Handsome's shoulder. A flirtatious laugh followed. Luke dug in.

"You'll be interested to know that the comely anchors once had a 'thing' in the late nineties."

"Chemistry is chemistry."

"His name is Steve Curtis. He went to Northwestern. His degree, luckily enough, was in communications. She went to USC, which is exactly where Southern California girls named Kimberly Lindell are supposed to go. Kimberly wanted to be a lawyer. Her dad was a lawyer. But an internship at a local television station led her to change her major from prelaw to communications."

"So that's why those two get on so well."

"Common ground fuels great relationships."

Steve and Kimberly were presenting a hard-hitting exposé on summer fashion. Steve dipped his index finger in zinc oxide and daubed it on his larger-than-normal nose.

"He's got a huge nose," I offered.

"It's really not that large — more Romanesque. In college, he grew a moustache as a diversion until a fraternity brother commented, 'If you want to divert attention from something, you shouldn't underline it.'"

The mood on set suddenly shifted. Steve Curtis and Kimberly Lindell simultaneously pressed their hands to their earpieces. Mr. FEMA was ready to go into the hole.

"Lucky for Steve the government guy is suited up," Luke said. "I was going to remind the world that he was once arrested in a West End bathhouse with a preop tranny named Minerva."

The grips finished securing the harness and stood ready to lower Mr. FEMA into the hole.

"You can't let the FEMA guy descend into the void nameless," I said.

"His name is Lloyd Keillor. He's married to stay-at-home mom Audrey. The happy union has produced four adorable children. Lloyd Jr., Frank, Joel, and baby Teresa. Lloyd has always worked in government. He began with the United States Postal Service but left because the mail was relentless. It just kept coming. He served a brief stint with the Department of Motor Vehicles but left after complaining that the pace was too fast. Lloyd found his comfort zone as a FEMA field rep. If you asked Lloyd Keillor what the world could use a little more of, he'd smile and say, 'Bureaucracy.'"

Segment producer Missy Wright counted down as Brock Robinson turned to the camera. At the same time, Lloyd Keillor flicked on the light atop his miner's helmet. The *Good Day, America* grips readied the crank and winch. Kevin Mackey dashed into frame with a flashlight. He stumbled to his knees and dropped the light, which rolled into the hole. RMWG flinched.

Silence.

Everyone waited to hear the flashlight hit bottom.

Nothing.

Brock observed that this was indeed a deep hole. Lloyd stared nervously into the abyss. He didn't really want to go in. Here came another flashlight. RMWG flinched again.

"Lloyd hates this part of the job," Luke continued. "He got into government because the workload was supposed to be light. He scored a nine-seventy on the SATs — a full forty points higher than President Decider. Right now, he's wondering why they don't lower *that* guy into a hole. That guy was in the National Guard. That's a government job. And president? Definitely a government job."

Lloyd didn't look good. He crossed himself and prayed. God would help him. Surely.

"The hole's got him praying?" Luke laughed. "God, that's funny!"

The pulley shifted to the right, and Lloyd Keillor flipped over. He was now heading into the hole — literally. A collective gasp came from the fans watching the monitors. Everyone on the set of *Good Day, America* held their breath. Even Bob Botty stared intently. The tepee steadied itself. It was a brief moment of terror, but all agreed that the shift in weight had stabilized the apparatus. They continued lowering Lloyd.

"God listens only to the president, dummy!" Luke

shouted. "Wait, God listens only to President Dummy, dummy!"

Then it happened. The tepee snapped. The ladders collapsed in on each other. The rope broke. Lloyd Keillor fell into the hole. The rope snaked after him. The *Good Day, America* grips raced after him. Brock spun to face his cameraman and Missy Wright, pointing again like a fascist dictator.

"The government worker fell into the hole? There's something you don't see every day," Luke said.

It was an oddly macabre scene. People panicked, scanned the hole for any sign of life. The producers cut to commercial in order to spare the viewing public. After all, children might be watching. What had begun as an opportunity to watch and applaud our government in action turned into a catastrophe of epic proportions. Fans called and texted friends to inform them of the tragedy they had just witnessed, live on the monitors in front of them.

"How long you think it'll keep him down there?" I asked.

"I don't know. You think it's a benevolent hole?"

Good question. How long was the hole going to keep an innocent man down? Michael Chapman was down there. Was he innocent? Actually, neither man was innocent. They both chose the hole — but for different reasons. Ultimately it didn't matter why. Chapman could have written his satire and turned his back on the hole. That's what J. D. Salinger did. Why did the quiet professor hire a publicist? Why did he sign with the Creative Artists Agency? Why did he take that three-picture deal with Paramount? His next novel was going to be a love story. What happened to that?

Lloyd Keillor's hole was a little different. He didn't allow himself to dream anymore. Lloyd Keillor was afraid to admit he ever had dreams. Dreams didn't come true for his kind. The Lloyd Keillors of the world bought magazines, watched movies, and channel-surfed. They suffocated in the dreams of others. Poor Lloyd Keillor.

"I hope it brings him back," I said.

"Are you pleading with the hole?"

"Everyone deserves a second chance. The writer had a shot. But Lloyd Keillor's like the hiker who fell into the mine — the guy they make a movie about, the guy who inspires everybody else to go after their fifteen minutes. A hiker falls into a hole, and everybody realizes how precious it all is. Lloyd Keillor should get a shot, you know, like the guy who recovers from cancer, the guy who has a near-death experience."

"Like the guy who gets hit by a drunk driver three days after his forty-fourth birthday, breaks every bone in his body — but lives."

"SOMOS LOS DIABLILLOS!"

The ground began to shake. Brock and his news team fled from the abyss. What was left of the winch and crank tumbled into the dark. The on-set audience screamed above the roar of an engine. They were screaming not for Lloyd Keillor, I realized, but because Bob Botty and rotund Charlie Arden were in the crowd, making contact with the mortals. The excitement thundered. We were witnessing the latest episode of *Mediocrity Gone Wild.*

Brock frantically pointed to the cameraman, shouting something the crowd drowned out. The only thing shaking more than the ground was the cameraman. He was terrified. He laid down the camera and ran for the safety of the van. There he dropped to his knees and turned his eyes to the heavens. What was Brock to do? He needed the shot. This was how anchors were made: wars, storms, big shaking holes. Then opportunity found Kevin Mackey. If he wanted to graduate to big-boy pants, he had to act. Kevbo picked up the camera. The power cable had pulled free. He tried to poke it back into its port.

"The same male-to-female connection," Luke said. "I bet he can't figure it out in time."

Kevin Mackey fumbled for a beat, then magically found the female connection. He hoisted the camera onto his shoulder and spun out in front of Brock. Thumbs up. Brock went to his mike.

Blinding lights shot out from inside the hole. Out leapt a huge, green safari Jeep. Mud flaps flying, top and windshield down — this bad boy had obviously been trekking across some serious terrain. Three tiny blurs inhabited the Jeep, which bounced wildly on two wheels, then righted itself. The green monster rumbled across the lot of the flagship Starbucks, spinning violently around to face the hole. The idling engine roared.

That's when I saw him. Lloyd Keillor was strapped to a stretcher that was tied to the roof of the Jeep. A tiny head wearing mud-stained goggles appeared from behind the steering wheel.

"Is *that* the driver?" Luke said.

The steering wheel was almost twice his size — this guy couldn't be any taller than eighteen inches, and he was screaming in a heavy Mexican accent.

"Hombre down! WE GOT AN HOMBRE DOWN!"

He jumped out and stormed over to the grips of *Good Day, America,* his jungle khakis making him look like a miniature British explorer. He directed the grips to the Jeep and shouted orders. In the Jeep stood two more tiny men in khakis. They jumped onto the roof and untied the stretcher. A black elf climbed to the end that supported Lloyd Keillor's head. An Asian elf followed suit. The Mexican elf pointed the grips into position, and Keillor was lowered to the ground. Then El Comandante ordered them to pull the front wheels of the FEMA ice-cream truck back to terra firma. They loaded Lloyd Keillor into the back of the truck as Mexican Elf pulled a map out of his back pocket and called the tallest of the grips to his side.

"Why do you think he chose the tall guy?" Luke mused.

"Height inspires confidence," I said.

"The only one in this whole shit-show who inspires any confidence is Señor Midget."

The little general explained something on the map. The tall grip nodded, and Mexican Elf snapped off a salute. The tall grip motioned the other mules into the truck, then climbed behind the wheel. The engine turned over, and "The Entertainer" began to play again. The FEMA truck rolled into the hole and disappeared.

Brock and Kevin Mackey shot the whole scene: the Jeep, the rescue, the tiny men in khaki pants. Brock moved in slow motion toward the leader. Kevbo had him full-frame. Mexican Elf walked with purpose. Brock walked with him. Thankfully the tiny commander's gait matched the intrepid reporter's.

"Sir? Excuse me, sir. Brock Robinson, Eyewitness News.

You just came out of the hole. Can you tell us what's down there?"

Silence from the tiny stick of dynamite with "Hecho en México" printed on his shirt and an American flag stitched over his heart. Brock needed to dig deep. He needed answers from the hero.

"Sir, why did you help the man who fell into the hole?"

That stopped El Comandante. His accent was heavy, but his English was remarkably good. "When a man falls down? Ju help him. Haven't ju ever read de Beel of Rights? All main are created equal. Ju don't let somebody who falls in de hole die like a dog!"

He started again, but Brock had one more question.

"Did you see anyone else down there?"

Mexican Elf spun. "Dere is a *lot* of people down dere. Dey deedn't fall. Dey're not dying. Dey're just *assholes.*"

The trio of elves marched past the monitor and made a beeline for Luke, me, and the green machine. In the monitor, I could see the backs of the elves — but not myself. The Chihuahua was there, the machine was there, but my desk, Luke's typewriter, and I were conspicuously missing.

Mexican Elf stood front and center. His tiny soldiers flanked him. Six tiny eyes stared up at me. Actually, three tiny eyes: Asian Elf wore a patch, which was very convincing, and Black Elf wore sunglasses.

"*Escritor?* Are ju de writer?" asked El Comandante.

They could see me?

"I am *a* writer," I explained.

The Hispanic leader extended his little hand. "*Somos los diablillos. . . .* We are de elves."

"The hole is on peyote." Luke snarked.

Asian Elf snapped the heels of his boots together, puffed out his chest, and gave a crisp salute. Black Elf saluted casually as he unwrapped a tiny stick of gum and offered me a piece. Now I understood the futility of offering a peanut to an elephant. Luke approached El Jefe, looking like a horse the little general might mount. Asian Elf took Luke's sudden movement as an act of aggression and jumped between them, executing a kung fu move — three quick punches followed by a roundhouse kick, all accompanied by a deafening scream.

"WHAT THE FUCK?" Luke shouted as he retreated.

"He's with me." I nodded calmly.

El Jefe stepped between the kung fu master and Luke, who was shaking now more than ever.

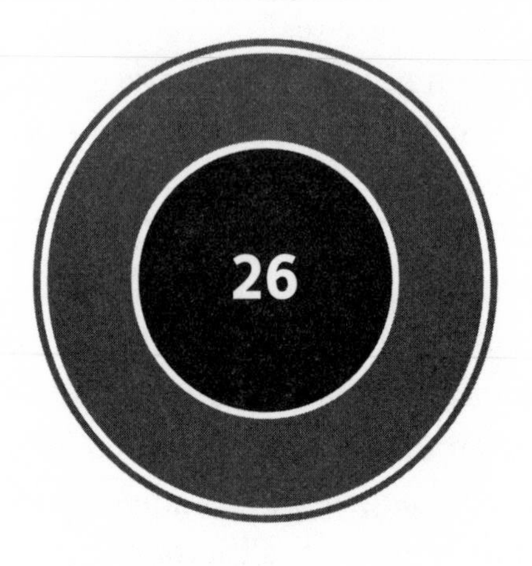

EL EXPLORADOR PEQUEIÑTO EXPLICA EL EXPERIMENTO GRANDE

"My name is Guerrero García," El Jefe said. "My friends call me G. Nacho G."

He introduced the black elf as Ice E.

"ICEE was the original Slurpee," Luke noted. "I think 7-Eleven stole the idea from KMart."

The kung fu master didn't like the digressions. You could see it in his eye.

"Dis is Choi," Nacho G said. "Just ignore him. He has a very short fuse when his blood sugar is low."

Choi opened his shirt to reveal a "Born to Lose" tattoo. Luke and I were more than a little intimidated. I imagined a tiny one-eyed boy held captive in some Shanghai sweatshop, forced to write misfortune cookies.

"We are cultural antropologists working in de field," G explained. "We have spent de better part of our careers traveling extensively throughout *el agujero* — de hole — tagging species and following dere migration patterns."

"Species?"

"*Sí,* humans. We have divided ju into subspecies: teachers, soldiers, real-estate agents, musicians, models, lawyers, i-bankers, housewives, atletes, actors, et cetera. De goal of our research is to track interaction wittin de hole."

"Really?" I said.

"Jess. Our study is being considered for de Cultural Horizons Prize."

"So what do I have to do with all of this?" I asked.

"Ju are de writer — not de hole, not de macheen. Dis story is coming from jor subconscious. Dis is de reason ju don't appear on camera."

"This world is real?" I asked, confused.

Nacho G looked out at the crowd, the flagship Starbucks, the set of *Good Day, America.* "*Sí,* it is very real," he said. "In de story, de writer does not exist. In de world, de story does not exist until it is moved by de creator. In dis world, ju are *el primum mobile . . . Cómo se dice?* . . . de prime mover. De writer. Just as ju cannot see de prime mover in jor world — de writer, God, whatever ju choose to call it. But dey do interact, as dey are one. Jor world, dis world, jor writer, our writer."

"But Michael Chapman could see me. OnStar Hal could see me."

"Ju as de writer chose dis digression. Ju alone divined it.

Ju brought us here to help wit jor friend. We tink he deserves a shot" — they all nodded in agreement — "and his fall may rouse him to live his dreams. But more important for us, four subspecies have mutated into aggressive new strains. We have tracked dem to dis area near de Starbucks. We must tag dem in order to continue our work and to keep de whole world from unraveling."

"What new strains?" I asked.

"The Rightist," said Ice E. "They're religious zealots, conservative, with a fanatically moralistic bent. Exclusively American."

"De Stalkarazzi," said Nacho G.

"I already know them," I said.

"Dere is a new type of celebrity, too," he said, "de celebutante. Reech, famous, mesmerizing, but wit no discernible talent."

"Worst," said Choi, "is new strain of game-show contestant we call reality-show contestant. If this population continue to grow in number, effect would be devastating. If we continue to treat world as one enormous talent show, idea of art and artist will cease to exist."

The tiny brow above Choi's eye patch started twitching. Was there another karate display on tap? He wobbled then toppled over face-first to the ground. No one moved.

"We should eat," Nacho G said. "Ju guys like tacos?"

THE WELL-ROUNDED TRIO

El Jefe's wife, Magdalena, put on one hell of a spread. She made the tortillas by hand. Strangely, the meal was full-size.

Nacho G met Magdalena — Spanish and normal-size — while on a fellowship at the University of Barcelona. They had trouble deciding whether they wanted to bring children into the world. On a recent trip through the hole, G witnessed a well-known female pop star and her dancer husband having sex on top of the Winnebago in the backyard of their Malibu mansion. The act occurred as the couple's child played with the dancer's two children from a previous marriage on a Slip'n Slide made of trash bags. Seeing this caused in him such an aversion to sex and children that the mere mention of coitus by El Jefe's wife sent him into a lengthy discussion of what he called procreation prophylaxis — everything from abortion and birth control to castration and emasculation. Minutes after witnessing the act, he actually took the morning-after pill.

They were very engaging, this trio of elves. They had met at Oxford University in a discussion group on the writings of J. R. R. Tolkien, C. S. Lewis, and Mervyn Peake. Choi weighed in, his tiny hands holding his full-size taco. In between bites he acknowledged his passion for art and architecture. He was particularly fond of impressionism and postimpressionism. He talked of Cézanne, Degas, and Gaugin, Manet, Monet, and Pizzarro, Renoir, Seurat, and Sisley, and — a favorite — Toulouse-Lautrec and Van Gogh. He admitted to having no understanding of Munch or Klimt.

Ice E's driving passion was the complexity of the relationship between pop culture and comparative religion. "Very simple people can create very complex problems," he offered. "It's such a tragedy that the entire world has been at war over the same god — the god of Abraham — with three different names."

His position that the cell phone was the twenty-first century's secondhand smoke was sublime, as was his comparison of rap with Enron or, better yet, the tech crash of 2002 — "The Emperor's New Clothes," he called it. "What a shame that this is where rap ended up," he said, "because in its humble beginnings the genre held so much promise. Where were the emperor's old clothes?"

There was nothing small about El Jefe's mind. When

Choi talked of art, Nacho G talked of art. Baroque, cubism, expressionism, fauvism, gothic, minimalism, neoclassicism, Renaissance — both Northern and Italian — Rococo, and romanticism. What the hell *was* the Italian mannerist period anyway? When Ice E talked religion, Nacho G shored up his argument with stories from world mythology, Native American folklore, and quantum physics. G was the smartest person under eighteen inches I'd ever met.

Hell, he was the smartest person I'd ever met, and he was right about the hole. The subspecies were mutating.

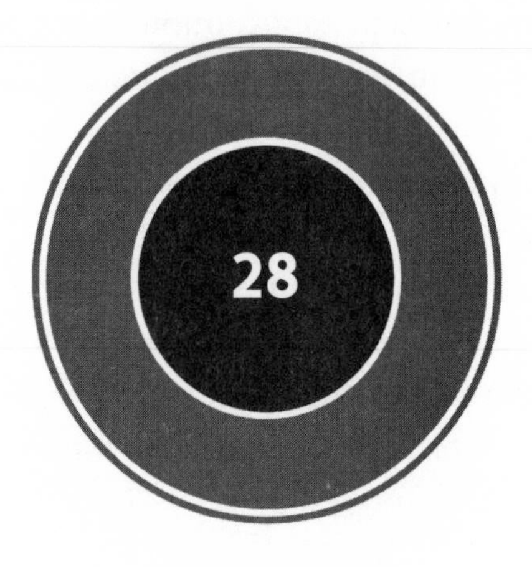

THE REALITY OF THE HOLE

The network had announced that they were auditioning for a new reality show to be shot in the hole. No sooner did the announcement air than a tram arrived from inside the abyss. It rolled up the ramp, at least a hundred people got off, and the vehicle descended back into the hole, quickly returning with another hundred people. The line around the sound stage was staggering.

G, Ice, and Choi unloaded their gear from the Jeep, piling it near the vending machine. The line of hopefuls spurred a discussion among the elves, Luke, and me. We all agreed that reality programming had long been an eyesore on the television landscape. We agreed, too, that it was cheap to produce and took relatively little creativity to market.

"As long as people continue to revel in the success of the everyman, it will endure," I said. "It reminds them that no matter how little control they feel they have in their lives, there is always an outside chance their voices will be heard."

"It's exactly that lottery principle that appeals to the masses," Luke added.

"*Sí,*" G said. "It is helty for de whole world to see ordinary people succeed. However, dere seems to be a new attitude to de phenomena occurring. De people no longer seem happy wit witnessing only success. It is de failures dat bring de most joy. It has become a culture of 'mean.' "

"When you feel so much anxiety about how little control you have at home, work, school, and the idiot talking too loudly on his cell phone," Ice added, "is it any wonder you refuse to give up the few feet of concrete your car controls on the highway? 'I don't care how long your blinker has been on, *muthahfuckah,* you're *not* getting in front of me. I'm in control!' Why shouldn't this attitude spill over to entertainment? Look at *this* jackass. He thinks he can sing?"

"Dey still like de weeners — not because dey ween but because dey make de losers look so bad," G said while surveying the gear.

When the hopefuls reached the front of the line, they auditioned for three people sitting at a table, who voted them in or out of the hole. Some hopefuls grew angry at the judges' decisions. Others were just so thankful that their dreams were almost fulfilled. One elated contestant jumped joyfully into the hole, and one particularly untalented candidate got an earful about just how bad he really was. G was right: everyone enjoyed this the most.

"What do you think they'll call it?" Luke said. "My vote's for *American Hole* — or maybe *America Sings Songs at the Hole.* The graphic could read 'ASS-Hole.' "

It was true. America was dying. In 1998 an audition process began for a reality program called *The Next American President.* It was cleverly promoted as a show by which anyone could take the reins of the country. They were looking for that boy or girl next door. *Remember that guy in your fraternity who was so funny? He could be president — and so could you!*

In November 2000 the final two contestants squared off in a battle for the ages. Americans went to their phones after the contestants' final performances. However, some voting viewers who supported the eventual runner-up heard a busy signal. There was talk of foul play. The runner-up was a dull kid who went on to win all kinds of awards as a documentary filmmaker. Turned out he was better off behind the scenes. When people learned that the winner was related to one of the producers, fingers really began to point — to no avail.

The Cowboy W Big Brother President's Show first aired in January 2001. The production team created a clever cartoon opening in which the new kid on the block rode in on a white horse, swinging his "W" brand wildly. He put his mark to the Constitution and burned it up like the map on *Bonanza.* The Nielsens went through the roof for the first few years — ratings unknown for network prime time — due in large part to several tragedies Cowboy W used to full advantage. One of his shining moments was a nationally broadcast cage-wrestling match where he beat up a town bully. When the bully pulled out a grenade with the initials W.M.D. stenciled on the side, Cowboy W lassoed him and brained him with his branding iron. Viewers later discovered that the grenade was carved out of soap that the bully had stolen from the local Best Western Hotel.

I hadn't watched the show in a long time. Actually, nobody was watching. Ratings had dipped to an all-time low. Producers hoped to combat this problem by promoting the slew of lovable characters that lived with Cowboy W at his D.C. house. There was Oil Can Dickie and Grandma Rummy. They were two dummies that sat on Cowboy W's knees. The dummies never moved their lips, of course. Only Cowboy W did. You had to give it to them, though. The dummies were good. If you looked hard, sometimes you could see the slightest movement, but when they drank a glass of water? Forget about it. And there was the gap-toothed tomboy estate manager who spoke only gibberish.

The show made a lot of mistakes during its run. One of the biggest was the network's decision not to renew the contract of one of the show's most popular characters. General POW!, a no-nonsense soldier, always tried to do the right thing but was constantly foiled by the bumbling antics of other characters. The show ran for eight seasons and was scheduled for cancellation in January 2009.

Just then a banner hawking an Eye Witness News Special Report interrupted *Good Day, America*'s segment "Dream

Closets: A New Home for Those 200 Pairs of Shoes." The waving banner gave way to national anchor David Hume. This had to be important. Behind him glowed a picture of the four chimps in suits. It was the end of Hal's video, the frame where the chimps hold poor Chapman over the hole.

Now to live video, full-frame. The four chimps were being arraigned in court. The judge read the charges. The chimps' attorneys whispered into the protruding ears of their clients. The chimp from the Creative Artists Agency pulled at his stifling collar. Paramount Chimp looked pissed. "Does this judge have any idea who he is talking to? My films have grossed over twenty billion dollars. I have a goddamn Academy Award!" The female chimp producer, a relative novice in the business, wondered why she had ever left the exciting world of accounting and finance. Male producer chimp looked worried. He liked white wine. He cut hair. In prison his name would be Debra.

Back to David Hume and a picture of the helicopter with a mystery man at the controls: a blacked-out face with a question mark in the center. Bravo, big-time news organization. Once again, a crackerjack graphic.

Nacho G carried an enormous — well, enormous for him — metallic case from the Jeep. Behind him marched Ice E and Choi, who had an even larger case hoisted high above their heads. G caught sight of the helicopter on the screen. He set the case down and went to one knee. Releasing the latches on the case, he opened it and removed a large gun with a considerable barrel. He had no problem handling the weight. He checked the sight and returned the gun to the case. Then he pulled out what looked like a photograph, which he presented to me.

"Ju assed me to bring ju dis."

"I did?"

It was a picture of Zoë. She was smiling, the sunset behind her. An uncontrollable sadness came over me. Why would I ask for a photograph of her? Of what did I want to remind myself? Zoë's smile made me feel again. I remembered the day I took the photograph. I remembered the time, what I was wearing, the food we were eating. I could see the year on the bottle of red wine we were drinking. I remembered because I was happy. There had been so few days that I was happy. I could remember every day because every day that I was happy was with Zoë.

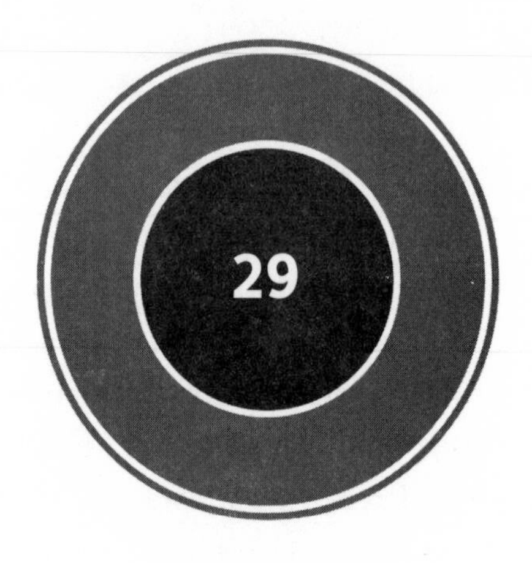

ABOVE THE CAFÉ IN ANTIBES

The picture was taken in the South of France. Zoë didn't like holidays. She referred to New Year's Eve as "amateur night." Christmas she dubbed the "day of familial dysfunction." She said she didn't remember the part in the Bible where Jesus came back from the dead to hide Easter eggs. Zoë liked to celebrate the "eves of the eves" of holidays.

February 12, 1992, was the first night I had ever spent outside the United States. I had just turned thirty years old. Paris was the most beautiful place I had ever been. It snowed. We walked along the Seine hand-in-hand, and I remembered that song from *The Sound of Music* that asks what you've done to deserve something so good.

Without Zoë I would never have seen movies like *The*

Sound of Music or *Breakfast at Tiffany's*. I would never have watched *Rebecca* or *Casablanca* or *Gilda* or *The African Queen*. I would have thought that *The Pride of the Yankees* was a sports feeling or that *An Affair to Remember* and *Indiscreet* were stories about infidelity. She opened my mind to everything: art and music, food and wine. I never read until I met Zoë. I was a liar and said I read, said I understood the complexities of wine, said I'd been to the Louvre. Zoë was the real deal. If she didn't know something, she asked. She wanted to learn. I wanted to be loved. I lied. Everything I had ever written since that first night on the beach was because of her. In everything I wrote she was there.

We climbed up to Montmartre, passing the artists and cafés. We shared a bottle of red wine on the steps of the Sacré-Coeur. She kissed me on the cheek as I looked out over the lights of the city. Until then, the Eiffel Tower had been only a picture on the calendar at the bike shop where I worked when I was seventeen. Now I was there. And I was happy.

That weekend we took the train along the southern coast, stopping in Antibes, a little village on the sea. We stayed at a small bed and breakfast called La Boquet. Our room overlooked an outdoor café. In the morning there was a fresh market in the village square. Zöe looked so beautiful in the morning light. She looked so beautiful as she read her book. I remembered how beautiful she was. I remembered.

She playfully kicked me under the table, then laid her leg against mine. I felt safe. She smiled over her book. "You know what?"

"What?"

"We should move here — when I'm done singing and you don't want to write screenplays anymore. We should move here, and you can write that novel."

"What novel?"

"The one about me and you and how I saved you."

I smiled. Zoë turned to the waiter and spoke in broken French. I loved that about her. No matter how much she thought she might screw up, she always dug in with both heels. She had a way of disarming you with her effort. The waiter was patient as he helped her pronounce word after word, nodding benevolently at her pronunciation.

"What did you say?"

"I think we're getting croissants with apricot jam. Although it is possible that I asked him to shank a lamb."

Every night, in bathrobes, we watched the sunset from the balcony of our room. We sipped red wine. We ate fruit and cheese with freshly baked bread. I told her how I loved her — how I loved her smile, her eyes. I told her how I'd loved her from the first time I ever saw her, when she was crying.

"I was crying because I hadn't met you yet," she said. "I was crying because it would be almost a year before we met. I will never cry again, because of you."

We stayed for ten days. Those were the happiest ten days of my life. The picture G gave me was from the balcony of our room above the café in Antibes in the South of France.

THE HOLY TORTILLA

Choi and Ice E sidled up to their leader. Together they held one of those plastic containers in which Mexican restaurants serve tortillas. It was enormous in their hands, like a manhole cover. G opened the lid of the tortilla cozy.

"What do you think?" Ice E asked.

G nodded and set the lid aside. He withdrew a full-size tortilla, holding it in front of him like a warm cornmeal beach towel.

"What you see?" said Choi.

Luke and I stared at the tortilla, really stared. I thought I saw a face. But it looked like the shadow face in the helicopter on the special news report.

"I know ju see someting."

"You know something juicy?"

"*Ay,* no. I know ju *see* someting."

"Oh. Um . . ." I made a wild guess. "The mystery man from the helicopter?"

That triggered it for Luke. "NO! Wait. . . . I see a face. . . . MAX VON SYDOW! It's Max von Sydow! From the Jesus movie!"

"*The Greatest Story Ever Told?*" I reexamined the tortilla. Oh. It *was* Max von Sydow. Max von Sydow as Jesus.

G nodded again. "Good work. Get de duffle."

"Are we right? Is it Max von Sydow?" Luke was wagging his tail in excitement.

"It is indeed acting great von Sydow. We juse his likeness as a releegious prototype. We place de image on a tortilla, cheese crisp, sometimes de wall of a jurinal. We chart de migration of people who come to pray to de vision. We will juse dis as a distraction for one of de Rightists today."

Choi and Ice E pulled an enormous green duffle from the Jeep.

"Dump dem next to de hole," G commanded.

They dragged the duffle to the edge of the hole, opened the zipper, and unloaded an immense pile of cameras and attachments.

"Owing to jor history wit de paparazzi, I look forward to seeing how ju bring dem from de hole," G said to me. "As a scientist, I try to report wit clarity, but wit dis strain — de stalkarazzi — I am ashame to admit dat I am prejudicial. Dey turn my stomach almost as much as de tought of de dancer and his pop-star wife making loff on dere mobile trailer." G reddened with anger. He really hated that dancer kid. He pulled his hunting rifle from the metallic case. "*Hombres!* Prepare jor weapons!"

Everyone knew my history with the paparazzi: I had taken Hunter's daughter, Camille, to the circus to celebrate her eighth birthday. Mom was playing in a celebrity poker tournament at some hip hotel in Vegas — the one with the big guitar out front. Camille had to go to the bathroom. The circus only had those Porta-Potty, Johnny-on-the-Spot deals. She was afraid to go in alone. I understood — it's dark inside. I went in with her and politely turned away. As she sat down, two clowns ripped open the door and feverishly shot pictures, chasing us out of the Porta-Potty and into the parking lot.

How do you stop an eight-year-old from crying while a man in a bright-orange wig flashes away? How do you stop an eight-year-old from crying as his hobo buddy baits you? You break Orange's nose, that's what you do. You break three of Hobo's ribs. Then you beat them into a month-long hospital stay. That will make the eight-year-old daughter of your poker-playing wife smile again.

How do they respond? With their own special brand of revenge. No need to hang you from the nearest tree when they have the Internet, *People* magazine, *Entertainment Weekly,* and *The Enquirer.* They hound you out of town with fire and pitchforks, clowns and hobos chasing you over the moat.

That's *my* reality.

THE CIRCUS OF THE HOLE IS PROUD TO PRESENT . . .

Starbucks Nation laughed and clapped as Bob Botty and the *Good Day, America* team did a makeup demonstration. Bob Botty's mechanical arms turned Serious Gretchen's face into a cat. Then the tin man turned Handsome into the scarecrow on his way to Oz. That zinc-oxide nose was the perfect starting point. Weatherman Charlie Arden was also applying makeup with the help of the *Good Day, America* beauty correspondent. She talked about makeup in the same tone most of us would reserve for the genocide in Darfur or Bosnia. In her defense, she did present the serious facts with a cheery "you know" as punctuation. Charlie and You Know applied makeup to Perky and Brock. They had pulled Brock off his live remote so You Know could demonstrate how easy it was to use makeup to accentuate your features. Lucky us. With some well-placed vertical lines of eyeliner, they turned Brock into a jack-o-lantern. Naturally.

There was joy on the set of *Good Day, America.* There was joy in Starbucks Nation as the reality hopefuls failed to become famous. It *was* a real circus. Luke laughed.

"What?" I said.

"Just thinking about the guns you gave the elves. You're gonna kill some paparazzi, aren't you?"

"No."

G hoisted the giant rifle over his back. How did this guy not fall over? Behind him, Choi and Ice E each carried their giant rifles with one hand. Choi used his free hand to snack on a candy bar. What was he going to be like on a sugar rush?

"De time is right," G said. "De paparazzi." Then, addressing Luke, "Dog, step away from de hole."

The lights on the set went down; the monitors went dark. Faces turned to their wireless lifelines. The judges had taken a break and were talking about the last horrific hopefuls.

"When you have acne that bad, you shouldn't even leave the house."

"It's certainly better than being fat."

"How 'bout the girl in the wheelchair? Can you imagine her in the hole?"

Nobody was watching. Time to bring in the paparazzi.

A voice came from inside the hole. I like this voice. No, I love this voice. It is charming and perfectly girlish. It is the voice of my wife's daughter, Camille. "Ladies and Gentlemen, please direct your attention to the center hole!"

"Who's that?" Luke said.

"Hunter's daughter."

"Camille? Wow. How old is she now?"

"Fourteen."

"Still lives with the grandparents?"

"Yeah."

"Grandma still addicted to painkillers?"

"Yeah."

"Grandpa still into white liquor and black girls?"

"Yep."

"Does this kid even stand a chance?"

"She does, actually. She's smart. She's beautiful on the inside. She's everything Hunter isn't."

Camille *was* beautiful. Camille was joy. Hunter didn't like Camille because she wasn't pretty enough. What did Hunter expect? Her dad was a junkie. OK, he was in a band. Same thing. He was five-foot-nothing and twenty years older than Hunter. He liked to beat her up. That made Hunter feel pretty on the inside. Hunter's dad used to be in a band. Hunter's dad used to hit her mom. So? They still went to church on Sunday. That made everything OK. Hunter was pretty on the outside and ugly on the inside — like the Republican Party. It looked good on paper. The agenda sounded good. But why were the Republicans so goddamn mean? What is it about religion that makes people so goddamn mean? — the extremists in the Middle East, the religious Right in the South, the northern conservatives, my grandmother. My grandmother went to church every day yet never had a kind word to say about anyone.

Calliope music began to play. Searchlights shot out from inside the hole, illuminating the starry sky of the sound stage. Then the hulk of an enormous cannon cranked its way, foot by foot, from inside the hole.

Camille's voice giggled. "Ladies and Gentlemen, the Circus of the Hole is proud to present the human cannonballs, Papa and Razzi! Excuse me —" The music stopped. Camille's voice rang like an announcement at the theater. "We normally ask that during the program you refrain from flash photography. However, for this performance, please feel free to shoot away!"

Luke looked back at me. "You're gonna launch the paparazzi out of that cannon so the elves can shoot them like skeet?"

I smiled. *"Pull!"*

BAM! The cannon unloaded with a white puff of smoke, a body sailing through the cloud. The figure flew through the air and crashed into the concrete wall just above the HOLLYWOOD sign, sliding to the ground like a cartoon villain. It hit the floor and rolled into the light. Bright-blue pantaloons, puffy yellow shirt, and a bright-red clown nose to compliment the bright-orange wig. Blood was streaming from the clown's ball nose. His makeup was covered in it. He pulled himself to his feet, his hand over his face.

"By doze! You broke by fugging doze! Fugging asshole! Where's by camera?" The clown looked all around him, finally spotting the pile of cameras. He walked through the line of reality hopefuls toward the hole. Nobody was looking. Nobody even noticed. That's reality for you. Here I was, giving them performance art, shooting clowns into a wall. If this were New York City, I'd have had my own special exhibit at the Guggenheim.

"You better dot have broken by camera!" the clown squawked.

"So the payoff is that there's no net?" Luke asked. "How many noses are you going to break?"

"I don't know. Maybe I'll break some ribs, too."

BAM! Another clown through the smoke and into the concrete.

"My ribs! You broke my fucking ribs! You fucking asshole! Where's my camera?" shouted the hobo clown. He, too, saw the equipment, crossed through the reality hopefuls, and walked toward the hole. Again, nobody batted an eye.

"You better not have broken my camera!"

BAM! BAM! BAM! Three more clowns flew out of the barrel. Three orange wigs slammed against the concrete. They all screamed in unison about their noses.

"I know, I know. . . . I'm a fucking asshole. I'd better not have broken your cameras."

BAM! BAM! BAM! Three hobos with broken ribs.

"Relax, I wouldn't break your camera. Cameras don't kill people. Cameras kill people who shoot pictures of people who shoot people from cannons."

All told, two dozen paparazzi hit the sound stage wall, with twelve broken noses and thirty-six broken ribs. It was better than sex.

THE WHORE OF THE CORN

The wounded clowns assembled with their cameras and attachments just outside the doors of the flagship Starbucks, off to the right behind a crowd barrier. The crowd in front of the Starbucks moved to the left of the door. The two barriers formed a path to the set of *Good Day, America,* along which a red carpet had been rolled out by the show's design team. It looked like a movie premier. *Who would I bring?* I thought.

One of the set decorators set up an easel behind the anchor's couch and propped up a movie poster. My stomach sank. It was a poster for Hunter's movie, *A Killer in the Corn ///.* She was on the promo circuit. Of course.

Luke and G zigzagged through the reality hopefuls. The audition process had resumed, and fans were smiling again at the tragedy of the process. Luke wasn't wearing his blue cardigan anymore. In place of the designer doggie apparel was the Max von Sydow tortilla, slung over his back like a saddle blanket. Both Luke and G were wearing radio headsets.

"Big Dog here is going *a la natural,*" Luke said to me. "You know, this tortilla keeps me surprisingly warm." He paused. "Why the red carpet?"

I indicated the monitor. The team was presenting a hard-hitting segment on divorce called "Ex-Games." He spotted the poster.

"Hunter?"

"Yeah. Fuckin' subconscious."

"It giveth, and it taketh away. You get clowns thrown into a wall, but then you also get the Whore of the Corn."

G cupped the microphone on his headset. "Ice, what's jor twenty?"

"In position on the roof of the news van. Over," Ice answered.

We all looked to the van, which was parked next to the *Good Day, America* rig. I didn't see him. "Where is he?"

"De satellite deesh," G said.

There he was. Ice was hiding behind the microwave arm inside the dish. He was so well hidden that his rifle looked like a piece of the dish's hardware.

"Choi, what's your twenty?"

"I on set. Over."

Over the radio came the voices of the *Good Day, America* team. An animal expert had just begun a segment on eccentric house pets, trying to put an unnerved Brock Robinson at ease with her maternal voice. She had perched a ferret on his shoulder.

"Oh, he won't bite."

"Do ferrets like pumpkins?" Weather Charlie joked.

"They like pumpkin seeds." Animal Expert was one of those people who never got the joke.

"I'm sure he'll ferret a few out from that big noggin!" Weather Charlie yucked as Animal Expert removed the terrified ferret from Brock's shoulder.

The crowd roared. Kimberly Lindell held a pot-belly pig in her arms. Steve Curtis had a large parrot with a tiny stuffed pirate on its back. Weather Charlie held the leash to a tiny caiman. Serious Gretchen was holding a terrified hairless cat. The crowd laughed. The anchors laughed. Weather Charlie put the tiny caiman on Brock's pumpkin head, upsetting the parrot but drawing applause.

"I in houseplant behind girl with naked cat. Over," Choi clarified.

I looked past Serious Gretchen's hairless pussy. Nothing. Then I spotted the top of Choi's tiny head behind a large waxy leaf. He peered slowly over the top of the plant and nodded. Then he quickly disappeared.

"*Team Reader?*" His whisper was frantic.

"Choi?"

"My position may be compromise. Over."

All eyes spun to the monitor. The naked cat had made visual contact. The cat squirmed from Gretchen's not-so-serious grip and scrambled over the couch. Baldy poked its head into the plant. Choi gave a short, tactical scream and executed three lightning-quick punches. "OI!" POP! POP! POP!

The demon cat yowled and ran like it had been electrocuted. The set roared with laughter.

"Watch out, kitty! Our plants bite!" Charlie Arden joked, milking it with another line: "Didn't that plant use to fight under the name Kid Ficus?"

Then Choi's confident whisper over the headset. "All clear."

"*Hombres,* prepare jor weapons. Let's not forget de rules of engagement. First visual contact. Clear de shot. Wait for my order."

G pulled a large military walkie-talkie from the stack of equipment next to the vending machine and marched it to me.

"I could juse jor eyes," he said, handing it to me. "We broadcast on nine. If at any time de op becomes compromise, we go to emergency ban five. Any questions?"

I shook my head.

G reached for the transmitter on his belt, flipped a tiny switch, and went to his headset mike. *Ksh.* "Check one, two." G's voice came loud and clear over the walkie-talkie.

"Check one, two," I repeated.

G gave me a tiny thumbs up, threw his enormous rifle over his shoulder, and turned to Luke. "*Perrito,* as we planned."

They moved for the doors of the flagship Starbucks.

"*Escritor,* remember, ju are de eyes of command central."

"Yeah. Um . . . I mean, uh, roger that."

"Is it so much to ask for the little general to call me by my first name?" Luke whined. "It's not bad enough you bring me back as a sacless purse pooch with a sombrero?"

"I can't tell him what to call you." I shrugged.

"Yes, you can. You're the *writer.*"

"Yeah, but . . ."

"Fine. I have an idea. What do you say, in the next act, to hoisting me up like a piñata? Give the guys from the local work-release program bats, and tell them there are hookers and cigarettes inside me."

"*Perrito!*" El Jefe had turned back to face us, looking impatient. Luke seemed, well, nervous. Then again, that was the trademark look of his breed, so what did I know?

"Wait — hey, sorry about the piñata thing, but . . . you're not gonna hurt me or anything? I mean — we're a team," he said.

"Of course I'm not gonna hurt you."

"I mean, these guys are pros. Look, when G first asked me to participate, I was pumped, but I think I was just caught up in the moment. I'm not sure I'm cut out for comb —"

"*Chihuahua!*"

"Morgan, I'm a pacifist." Luke was shaking.

Nacho G marched back to Luke. "It is on de battlefield where legends are born. Look at dis test as a call from de gods for ju to take jor true place among de panteon of great warriors. It is jor destiny to rise above what it means to be merely mortal! It is jor destiny to reach inside and find de mettle to be great! It is jor *destiny,* CHIHUAHUA!"

THE OFFENSIVE FOR STARBUCKS NATION

Man, El Jefe knew what he was doing. He was like a mini Patton standing on a tank. I could have pulled my arm right out of its socket — that's how badly I wanted to follow him into action. Luke was fired up. He reared up on his hind legs. His fierce growl became a fierce bark. The shaking pacifist was no more. The grizzled commander guided the neophyte soldier onto the battlefield.

Until now the story had been unfolding from my subconscious. However, owing to the capricious nature of same, G suggested that for the duration of the offensive I dictate the narration manually. I understood his position. I'd been there before. In Hollywood, this method is called "budget constraints." G and Team Elf could ill afford mistakes. G assured me that after the battle had been won, I would be free to turn the reins back over to my whimsical inner mind.

I surveyed the sound stage. The barrel of Ice E's rifle protruded from the satellite dish. Kevin Mackey and Segment Producer Missy Wright climbed into the van, ignorant of Ice and the impending offensive. The clowns stood ready with their cameras. Starbucks Nation was watching the monitors, on which glowed Steve and Kimberly and the *Good Day* gardening correspondent. They were demonstrating how to pot a new houseplant. Gardening Gal checked their work. *Good job!* I counted six new hiding places for Choi and his peaking sugar high. G took his position atop the flagship Starbucks.

The planned offensive called for implanting eight identification tags. The strike would occur simultaneously on the four targeted groups. One reality show hopeful and one stalkarazzo were to receive a tag; they were the responsibility of Ice E. His marksmanship would be needed in sedating the lone celebutante entering via the red carpet. The Rightist and the other five celebutantes were to receive the final six tags. The celebutantes would receive the greatest number of tags due to the enormous variation of celebrity within the mutated strain. Four celebutantes were to be tagged on the set of *Good Day, America,* the fifth outside.

I heard G over the radio as he took his position: the offensive would begin with Luke making his way into the audience. With all eyes on the monitors, Luke could slip in unnoticed. He would shake the von Sydow Jesus tortilla free, making sure the corn treat was face up. The purpose of the corn Von Sydow was simple: with nothing to draw the attention of Starbucks

Nation, their limited minds would wander. Most would find their cell phones or crackberries; others would think about how their personal music libraries defined them as individuals. However, the Rightist, with his limited brainpower, had a tendency to forget that technology existed at all. He occasionally acted as though he had unexpectedly traveled back in time — sometimes up to fifty years. When he found that he couldn't locate his Bible, he would turn his gaze skyward in prayer, which could compromise the positions of both G and Ice. The hope was that the tortilla would be discovered by another Rightist who was looking down his nose at society. Once Luke's work was done, he would make his way back to my position.

Nacho G would initiate the strike by taking out the power grid that controlled the lights on set. Ice and Choi would have less than ten seconds before the backup generator brought *Good Day, America* back on line. That was how much time they had to complete the assault. All that was left was for me to write the scene that would bring the celebrities to the set. My subconscious mind had decided on Hunter's movie. Now I had to execute the scene consciously.

In subconscious writing you see the character. The conscious process of writing begins with seeing the actors. Most people in Hollywood write consciously. This is due in large part to the recent phenomenon of the movie star–producer. You write for the actor, not the character. Movie stars do not want to be seen in anything but the perfect light, so the complexities that make great characters are forbidden.

Actors are like sheep. Making movies is like tending a flock. There are three acts in a movie and likewise three aspects to making a movie. First, you write the screenplay — that is, you decide what the sheep will say. Second, you shoot the movie, or herd the sheep through the pasture as they say what they are told to say. Third, you edit the movie, or shear the sheep to make them presentable for sale. The sheared wool becomes those "special features" that make buying the DVD so appealing.

Sheep are easy to control. A good border collie can keep them in line. Some sheep become stars. They are more difficult to control. They become sheep in wolves' clothing. To control them you need to be in their confidence. You do this by coddling the wolves. Indulge the wolves. Flatter the wolves. You need to find the sheep they used to be. When the shooting is over, you shear the wolves.

Sheep travel in droves. Wolves travel in packs. At the Academy Awards, the drove applauds the pack. Then you start all over again.

I needed a set, an interior. They couldn't just arrive on the red carpet. They were sheep. I needed a set where I could be conscious of the actors. A greenroom. I'd bring the actors from the greenroom. A greenroom is a show-business waiting room. Every television show has a greenroom. It's where actors congregate, do a line of blow, have a glass of wine, or nibble on something at a high-class craft service table. The greenroom. The paddock for the sheep. I know who I will bring in on the red carpet — the wolf.

My free hand reached for the keys of the typewriter, which were were warm and vibrating faintly. I loaded a clean sheet of paper into the carriage and began to type.

INT. GREENROOM — DAY.

A TALENT COORDINATOR pokes her head into the greenroom. Seven ACTORS are laughing and joking around the craft service table. Four women, three men. They are model types: tan with perfect bone structure. They range in age from 18 to 29. They look to the talent coordinator who gives instruction.

TALENT COORDINATOR

When we come out of commercial, Kimberly and Steve will introduce the seven of you. You'll sit on and behind the couches.

Excited and nervous laughter from the actors.

TALENT COORDINATOR

(continuing)

Nikki and Dakota, you'll sit between Gretchen and Steve. Jake and Ethan between Kimberly and Charlie. Emily,

Kate, Master Z, and Topher will sit on the stools behind the couch. Kimberly will introduce a clip, and then Hunter will arrive. We'll put Hunter in the middle between Steve and Kimberly. And guys? Remember to smile.

CUT TO:

Remember to smile? It was hard to smile with Hunter in the middle. Actors from the greenroom, Hunter from the hole.

G's voice came over the walkie-talkie. *Ksh.* "*Escritor?* De scrip says dey will bring on de actors and den introduce a cleep. How will ju bring de wolf from de hole?"

"I'm working on that."

"Let us know when ju are ready to shoot."

How would I bring Hunter from the hole? How would Hunter want to enter? Hunter would never come from the greenroom. Hunter was a star. The audience always wants a big entrance from a star. Like that five-foot-six action star — he would ride a motorcycle out of the hole, climb off his bike, and step onto his soapbox. Then he'd be six-foot-two. Talking about depression and other life lessons is always more effective coming from tall people. Height inspires confidence. How did he know that? Maybe he was smarter than the rest of us.

Again I attacked the keys of the IBM Selectric.

INT. / EXT. HOLE — NIGHT.

Wind begins to swirl. We hear the thundering blades of a helicopter. Rising out of the hole is the chopper. We've seen this monster before. It is the same craft that ordered the chimps to throw Michael Chapman into the void.

CUT TO:

EXT. STARBUCKS — SAME.

The helicopter lands next to the red carpet. The AUDIENCE turns with great anticipation. The PHOTOGRAPHERS ready their cameras. The door of the chopper opens. HUNTER steps out onto the red carpet. She waves. The audience goes crazy. The photographers wrestle for the best position to take her picture. Flashes of light fill the air. Hunter waves while posing for photographers at the same time.

CUT TO:

INT. GOOD DAY, AMERICA SET — SAME.

The AUDIENCE stares excitedly at HUNTER arriving on the red carpet. STEVE and KIMBERLY look into the cameras.

STEVE

It looks as if our mystery guest is making a perfect megastar entrance.

KIMBERLY

Would you expect anything less?

Hunter steps through the doors of Starbucks and onto the set of Good Day, America. She waves into the camera, crosses to the couch, and hugs Steve and Kimberly with false affection. She kisses BOB BOTTY. She waves hello to the ACTORS as well as CHARLIE and GRETCHEN. The audience is going wild. She blows a kiss to them. Steve invites her to sit.

STEVE

Hello, Hunter. Welcome back.

CUT TO:

"We're ready to shoot," I said into the walkie-talkie.

Ksh. "Roger that," G said. "Good work, *Escritor.* Ice?"

Ksh. "Yes, Team Leader?"

Ksh. "Let de wolf clear de first row of photographers and get to de door. I'll knock out de lighting grid from my position here on de roof, and ju take her down."

Ksh. "Roger that."

Ksh. "Choi?"

Ksh. "Yes, Team Reader."

Ksh. "De target celebutantes, code-named Dakota and Jake, are de female and male subjects just off de shoulders of de hosts, code-named Steve and Kimberly. De tird target is code-named Topher. He will be on de fardest stool to jor right. Target four is code-named Master Z. He will be left of code-named Topher."

Ksh. "Roger that."

G had targeted Hunter for obvious reasons. She had become a megastar based on who she was: rich, family name, no discernible talent. It fit the anthropologists' criteria for the experiment. She didn't come up through the ranks of the oppressed. Her art wasn't shaped by pain or injustice. Hunter had no desire to change the world. She just wanted to be famous. So there was a sex tape. Publicity was publicity. G wanted to prove his hypothesis that this new breed of celebrity would destroy art as we knew it by having no base by which to create it. Hunter was the perfect choice to shoot.

Dakota did have some talent — but no passion. She just happened to be at the mall on the day that the show that makes stars out of singers was there. She can sing. But should she be in a movie? She had a perfect voice but no soul. Starbucks Nation bought that perfect song from their local music megastore, and Dakota became a pop star.

Jake had a reality show on one of the music channels. He pulled stunts like letting people kick him in the balls or push him down a flight of stairs in a shopping cart full of broken glass.

Topher finished third place on a reality show where they continually humiliated the contestants. He was eliminated, in tears, at the end of an episode on which he was buried up to his neck in human feces and challenged to eat a platter of glazed doughnuts. He could eat only seventeen. He may not have won the money, but he was better-looking than the winner.

Master Z was a popular rap "artist" known for his harsh urban lyrics. His fame came from a number-one hit that used ten or so notes from a hugely successful rock song from the seventies. The rock song was the hook. His generation calls it sampling. Everyone else calls it copyright infringement, plagiarism, and theft. People loved him right out of the box. He carefully cultivated his rebellious art. What nobody knew was that Z's real name was Anthony. His father was an actor, and his mother was an economics professor at Stanford. Anthony "Master Z" Ford was a fraud. His cornrows were a fraud. That grill on his teeth was a fraud. Anthony was an Emile. Mommy and Daddy loved him so much that they let him be urban. They let him pretend to be a gangsta — if that helped him express who he thought he was. These new stars were willing to humiliate themselves to make us feel better about ourselves, and we loved them for it.

Ksh. "Choi, jor tags are code-named Dakota, Jake, and Master Z. After I tag code-name Hunter on de carpet I'll crash de doors and tag code-name Topher, but ju need to sedate him. Hit him second and wit a few more CCs. He's a big boy. He can handle it."

Ksh. "Yes, Team Reader."

Ksh. "We'll rendezvous at de macheen. Chihuahua?"

Ksh. "Yes, Team Leader." Luke's voice quivered with excitement.

Ksh. "Lights up. Clip introduced. Step into de crowd. Tortilla onto de ground. Retreat to de green macheen," G instructed.

Ksh. "Team Leader? Why is it rendezvous for you guys and retreat for me?" Luke asked.

Ksh. "CHIHUAHUA!"

Ksh. "Sorry, Team Leader. Max von Sydow faceup. Retreat to machine. Got it."

The elfin anthropologists worked like a well-oiled machine. Science and culture couldn't be in safer hands.

We agreed to wait for *Good Day, America* to come out of the next commercial interlude before striking. There was always the possibility of the all-too-common double dip that morning shows execute when they come out of commercial, tease you with a story, and dive back in to another bank of advertising. This bothered Luke, who was impatient for the operation to begin.

Lights, camera, action: Kimberly and Steve joked with Charlie. Serious Gretchen sat on the couch, giggling with Brock Robinson, who sat beside her. That wasn't in the script. Brock Robinson was beyond my control. The character had discovered celebrity, which meant bad news for any writer. He had found his comfort zone. Any idea of serious journalism now seemed only an afterthought to him. Brock liked using his resolute reporter persona to comment on everything from the latest technology trends to the hottest new video game. Why should he try bringing integrity to the world of television reporting while everyone else had all the fun? Serious stories like the hole could wait. There were more important topics to discuss. Big stories, like the hottest celebrity download of the week. The book written by that heiress's dog. Who wasn't interested in two movie stars and their baby? They were naming the child *what?* Hey! Guess what the hottest tattoo will be this summer. The pop star who was like a virgin found God. Wait, she's a Jew? But in all her videos she was writhing in a Catholic church. Thankfully, the celebrity press would sort out all the confusion.

Ksh. "Escritor?" G was on the roof, staring down at the monitor. "De pompkeen isn't in de original draft."

"He doesn't seem to want to leave," I said.

Ksh. "He is in Choi's sight line for code name Topher."

I didn't know what to do. What would G want me to do? Brock was a celebrity now. I'd lost control of him as a character. I was trying to write consciously, but he wasn't responding.

Ksh. "Choi?"

Ksh. "Yes, Team Reader."

Ksh. "After ju sedate code-name Dakota, take Brock down and tag him — code name Big Squash. Den Jake and Master Z."

Choi offered a small suggestion. *Ksh.* "Team Reader, if I must fire five round, I suggest you tag Big Squash. For proximity reason."

Ksh. "*Bueno.* I'll take code name Big Squash. Hit him wit de last round. Amp de CCs."

Ksh. "Yes, Team Reader."

Ksh. "*Escritor?*"

"Yes, Team Leader?"

Ksh. "Bring de actors from the greenroom, sit dem on de couches, and introduce de cleep. We're ready for *la puta del maíz.*"

"Yes, Team Leader."

READY, AIM, SEDATE

Kimberly and Steve welcomed the sheep from the paddock. Brock fit right in as he kissed the women and shook hands with the men. Each sheep sat in its predetermined space on couch or stool. Pleasantries passed back and forth as each celebrity relayed a little story about the movie. The real question, though, was how each one liked working with a megastar like Hunter. Seven answers expressed one thought: "It was, like, really awesome." Time to introduce the clip.

Perky faced the camera. The audience waited with baited breath for the first tantalizing look at a future summer blockbuster. The clowns stood at the ready, breathing painfully, blood dried on their makeup.

Perky read perfectly from the teleprompter. "The biggest

buzz out of Hollywood this summer surrounds the movie *A Killer in the Corn III,* starring Hunter O'Neill. It's the third picture in the franchise based on the megahit from nineteen seventy-nine. A girl with telekinetic powers inadvertently summons the devil to her sleepy Midwestern town. Here's an exclusive first look at the thriller."

The audience shivered with anticipation. The sheep applauded themselves. There was Hunter racing through a cornfield.

Ksh. "Cue Chihuahua," G ordered.

Luke stepped into the light wearing the Max von Sydow Tortilla. He walked directly into the crowd in front of the monitors.

Ksh. "Chihuahua, two steps to jor right. Drop de tortilla next to de couple in de 'Country Music jUSA' jackets. Can ju see dem?"

Ksh. "You mean the black satin jackets? I can't read them. The jackets with the eagle and American flag?"

Ksh. "Sí."

A pause.

Ksh. "The tortilla has landed. I repeat, the tortilla has landed. Chihuahua retreating to machine." Luke walked across the red carpet past the clowns. No one even noticed him.

Ksh. "Cue helicopter."

Chopper blades rose from the hole and pounded the air. I felt an inordinate sense of dread. I didn't want to see Hunter. She'd have that "I just got fucked and strangled" look. What if the stunt man is with her? I'm the writer. Would I do that to myself? Sure I would.

The helicopter rose from the abyss. The sound was deafening, yet the audience and clowns didn't seem to notice. The last time the helicopter was on site someone commanded four chimps in suits to throw Michael Chapman into the hole. Who would be thrown in this time? Would anybody care? Probably not. Celebrities were on set.

The clip ended. The audience couldn't believe their luck. This movie would *definitely* live up to the buzz! The sheep congratulated each other. What terrific work they'd done. Wait. Steve Curtis announced a surprise guest. A mystery silhouette appeared on the monitors with a question mark at its center. Another crackerjack graphic! Stay tuned!

The helicopter flew across the night sky of the sound stage, touching down smoothly next to the red carpet. The audience turned from the monitors with great joy. The clowns crowded in for the shot. The more they pushed and jostled each other, the more pain spread across their faces. Knowing that cameras were being pushed into smashed noses and ribs almost made it tolerable that Hunter was about to appear.

The door of the helicopter sprang open. Hunter's entourage spilled onto the carpet. It didn't matter that it wasn't in my script. I had no control over Hunter's world. Her agent, hair stylist, life coach, makeup artist, manager, personal assistant, personal chef, Pilates instructor, publicist, and stunt man escorted the great bundle of joy who had never wanted for anything in her whole life onto the red carpet. Maybe one of the helicopter blades could dip and cut Hunter's halo off.

No. I didn't want to kill her. Yet.

Cameras flashed, and the audience collectively frothed. They believed they were in the presence of real talent. Hunter waved. She really knew how to work the crowd. She looked coquettishly over her shoulder and back at the wall of clowns. Hunter really knew how to take a picture, too. In moments, Operation Starbucks Nation would commence.

One final kiss for her fans, one more pose for the clowns. *Good Day, America* prepared to welcome American royalty.

Ksh. "Ice, ju in position?"

Ksh. "I have visual contact. Hunter is in my sights."

Ksh. "Choi?"

Ksh. "Visual contact estabrished. I good to go."

Ksh. "*Hombres,* let's do dis for Darwin!"

G sighted the transformer atop the light post between the hole and the flagship Starbucks. BAM! It looked like a bottle rocket shot out of the barrel. *Bull's-eye!* The transformer exploded in a shower of electric sparks, followed by an electrical hum and popping lights. *Good Day, America* went dark.

Ksh. "GO, GO, GO!"

The cameras on set were still live. Only the lights had short-circuited. You could still see the silhouettes of the actors and hosts on the monitors.

Ice fired a perfect shot into Hunter's ass. God, I hoped she really was down, because any sharp poke in Hunter's ass always led to rough-and-tumble horseplay. Once she got a look at the handsome eighteen-inch Latino, well, I'm afraid Nacho G would be in danger of being lost forever. G fired a shot at the guy in the country-music jacket. *Pop!* A perfect shot into his shoulder. Their accuracy was stunning.

Ice leapt from the satellite dish and disappeared into the line of reality hopefuls. G leapt from the roof, over the red carpet, and into the audience. The country-music lover fell to the ground as if his legs had been kicked out from underneath him.

"Wow . . . They're *fast* little fuckers," Luke said, then scurried closer for a better look. "Mother of God! He dropped Country-Music Guy right onto the Jesus tortilla! Hey, Hunter's tit is out!"

Ksh. "CHIHUAHUA! Retreat to de macheen!"

There were a pop and a beep over the walkie-talkie — the signal that a tag had been applied successfully.

Hunter was most definitely down. The clowns were frantically shooting the scene — a celebrity in a compromised and humiliating position. One of Hunter's breasts had pulled a Janet Jackson. Had to get it on film. This one shot would buy a condo in Boca.

G was something, all right. He was next to Hunter only for a split second. He pressed against her shoulder the small gun that inserted the tag. Over the walkie-talkie came another pop and beep. In one fluid motion, he stood, ran, and crashed in a barrel roll through the doors of the flagship Starbucks.

Ice was atop a reality hopeful. *Pop, beep.* He ran for the phalanx of clowns, dropped to one knee, and aimed his enormous rifle.

Click. Nothing.

Ksh. "Team Leader, I have a jackal at position three. Weapons jam."

Ksh. "Keep visual contact until problem resolved," G responded.

Ksh. "Roger."

Ice did his own barrel roll and took up a position against a wall behind the clowns.

Choi executed his offensive splendidly. Four shots came over the radio. BAM! BAM! BAM! BAM! Dakota, Jake, Master Z, and Topher all toppled. Another shot. BAM! Pumpkin Brock wobbled like a bear that wasn't ready for spring. Choi jumped out of the houseplant, landing next to Dakota. *Pop, beep.* The doors crashed open, and G raced for Big Squash. Choi stood on Jake. *Pop, beep.* Brock Robinson suddenly flipped onto his back. Now I understood how Country-Music fell. Just an elf and his rifle.

Pop, beep. Choi jumped off Topher.

Brock struggled on the floor. G couldn't get a clear shot to apply the tag. Choi ran to G's aid, screaming in sugary delight.

"OIIAHH!" Three quick strikes. TCH! TCH! TCH! *Pop, beep.* Big Squash Brock Robinson had been tagged. Choi and G turned for the doors as the set lights began flickering back on. The pint-size trio was dangerously close to running out of time.

Ksh. "Ice?" said G.

Ksh. "Weapon still jammed."

Ksh. "We're on our way."

The lights began to come up. On the monitors were the smiling faces of the actors and the *Good Day, America* team. They had survived the great blackout. Hunter was standing at the door, still on the red carpet. It appeared that she only tripped in the dark. She secured her tit, clowns shooting away.

G and Choi ran undetected through the doors and under Hunter. They scampered across the red carpet and around the clowns. They'd only taken thousands of pictures so far, but wasn't the last one always the best?

G and Choi were out of sedative. G had used the reserve on Brock. They agreed to take down one of the stalkarazzi manually. The trio always carried one shot extra in case of such an emergency, but two guns jamming in the same op was almost mathematically impossible. G swung the butt of his rifle at the feet of a clown who had turned away from the group to load film. BAM! Bozo landed on his back. "OOII-IAHH!" TCH! TCH! TCH! Ice calmly applied the tag. *Pop, beep.* The trio climbed from the bloody painted beast and ran for the rendezvous at the Starbucks drink dispenser.

Mission accomplished.

CONFLICT RESOLUTION

Good Day, America welcomed the Whore of the Corn. Kisses, hugs, and hellos. Everyone loved America's sweet tart. Did she hurt herself? Let's hope not. Precious cargo en route to the couch. There was only one obstacle: Pumpkin Brock was still laid out. Someone had a little too much punch! Choi's specialty punch, that is.

We were beginning the third act: the resolution of the conflict. Hunter sat. The actors *baa*-ed to their goddess. Perky and Handsome chatted with the muse of the common people. Bob Botty rolled his gyroscope behind her. Weather Charlie and Serious Gretchen wanted to talk about Hunter's perfume line: like nectar from the gods. Could a treat so delightful ever find the soft, red tongue of Randy Samples? She almost seemed to glow.

Hunter was one of the leaders of the new culture, a culture, as G had remarked, where nobody actually created art. People like Hunter had removed the artist from the art. There were no da Vincis or Mozarts anymore. No Tolstoy, Proust, Nietzsche, Joyce, Hemingway, Dostoevsky, Dickens, Cervantes, Brontës, or Austen. Big Dick had been turned on its head. The poet was dead, replaced by a rich teenager with a rhyming dictionary.

The line of reality hopefuls was still growing. Voltaire was right. What was too silly to be said was perfect to be sung. The world had turned into one giant talent show. Thumbs out of your asses, up or down for latest trend. Sad thing was you didn't need talent to win. People with talent wouldn't dare show up at the audition. That would be compromising their art. Culture was dying. I would have liked to think I was above it all, but I was part of the problem. *The Chihuahua in the Blue Prada Bag?* Fuck me.

I met Hunter at the 1993 Sundance Film Festival. She wasn't the star she is today. That was before the obsession with celebrity became a global phenomenon, before the Internet boom, before the rise of the everyman as critic.

Luke and I flew in from Los Angeles. Zoë was in New York celebrating her parents' twenty-fifth wedding anniversary. The next day a blizzard shut down all the airports. Zoë missed the premier of the movie of which I was reminded every day. After the premier, *GQ* magazine hosted a party. It was there that I met Hunter.

Hunter was beautiful, rich, and supremely confident. She was the life of every room she entered. Everyone loved Hunter. She was perfectly mannered, perfectly tailored, perfectly perfect. Luke's father had dated Hunter's mother in the early sixties, before Hunter's mother met and married the handsome alcoholic with a closet case of jungle fever.

I liked the attention from Hunter and her friends. I liked the way Hunter flirted with me, the way she flipped her hair as she playfully pushed my shoulder. The weight of her leg against mine didn't make me feel safe the way Zoë's did. It made me feel — famous. I liked the way the photographers circled our table like sharks. I wrote the movie where the guy throws his glove through his girlfriend's windshield. I *was* the guy who threw the glove through the windshield. I cheated on Zoë that night. My heart stopped when Hunter, naked, answered my door to find Zoë on the other side. Zoë wasn't due to arrive for another day, but she found a way to get to Utah. I wanted to cry as I remembered this, but I didn't cry.

Luke died a month later, killed on Mulholland by a twenty-two-year-old drunk driver. Zoë attended the funeral but left without speaking to me. I chased her, shouting her name, wanting to cry. I didn't cry.

Seven years passed before I spoke to Zoë again. I saw her at LAX. I met her husband. I was devastated. As she walked away, she looked back at me. I thought, *I love you,* and she looked at me the same way she had looked at me the night we took our first walk on the beach. Two months after seeing

Zoë for the first time in seven years I married Hunter. The circus attended. My best man asked me before the wedding why I was marrying someone who made me so miserable. "Because I hate myself," I answered. How's that for conflict resolution?

My best friend and the love of my life were gone. After Luke's funeral, my heart stopped forever. I willingly turned the reins of the story back over to my subconscious with one final thought: LET'S END THIS. I wasn't interested in Hunter's new cell-phone video game. The clowns, the reality hopefuls, the audience, all the members of Starbucks Nation, I was no longer interested in their story. They were all prisoners of whim.

Time to write the third act.

I suddenly felt free. Disentangled, unencumbered. I no longer knew what I wanted, and I didn't care. I finally gave up control. A familiar feeling washed over me. I'd been here before. I used to feel this way when I wrote. With Luke. Before the limos. Before the parties. Before Hunter. With Zoë. I'd forgotten.

I began to think of all the feelings I'd forgotten. I'd forgotten that Zoë reminded me of a cat. I'd forgotten that I gave up my apartment and moved in with her. Until Luke reminded me, I had forgotten the boat, *Zoë's Rose Tattoo.* I'd forgotten Zoë couldn't cook. I'd forgotten how Zoë used to joke that she was the only person who could burn a salad. I'd forgotten we ordered in every night. I'd forgotten Zoë loved pizza. I'd forgotten how much I loved sleeping with Zoë. I loved how we would lie on our sides with our faces inches apart. How we would whisper in the dark. I'd forgotten her whisper.

"You know what?" she said.

"What?"

"What do you think of the name Ava? I mean, if we ever had kids and we had a girl, Ava is such a pretty name, and Ava Gardner was so beautiful. What do you think?"

"I like it, but with your track record with cooking, don't you think —"

"I don't think even I could screw up breast-feeding. After that, we'll hire a Mr. Belvedere or an Alice."

"A TV character?"

"You want her to be entertained, don't you? That's why they invented TV — for people who are hungry."

"Is that why I like TV so much?"

"You're the one who wanted to order from the Tea Garden. I told you the portions were small."

I'd forgotten how I used to push the hair from her face.

"I love you."

I'd forgotten how I loved to stare into her eyes. I'd forgotten how I thought to myself that I never wanted that feeling to go away.

"If we ever have a daughter, I hope she looks just like you."

I'd forgotten how much I loved to kiss her.

"I hope she doesn't cook like you, though."

I'd forgotten her laugh, that laugh I loved. I'd forgotten she liked to sleep on my side of the bed. I'd forgotten how I loved Zoë's body. I'd forgotten that it was perfectly imperfect. She complained about her hips, her breasts. I loved them. I loved the sight of her wearing my underwear. I loved her in that black bra and white tank top. I'd forgotten that Zoë had no tattoos. Her band, Zoë's Rose Tattoo, was a joke. I'd forgotten she was afraid of needles. She confessed that while her friends were getting their bodies inked she had put her tattoo money in the bank. She was saving up to buy a cottage where she could hang the art that she would buy when traveling the world.

How could I forget that? How could I forget that she loved to sing? How could I forget Zoë? How could I *forget?*

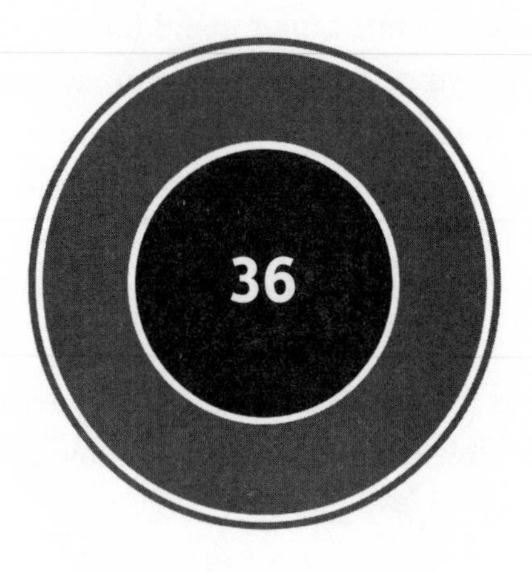

THE DREAM OBSERVED

G, Choi, and Ice were loading gear back onto the Jeep. It felt good to have no responsibility to my characters anymore.

The clowns were still standing in line. The reality hopefuls were still lining up. Country-Music was staring down at the Jesus tortilla. Hunter was explaining her new video game, which you could play on your phone. The actors laughed as they looked down at their new toys.

"It's called *Night of the Hunter.* For the girls, you can be a sassy spy or a rich socialite assassin or a slut with a gun. The boys can be gangsta rappers or mafia hit men or hip-hop dancer spies."

"I'm going to be a slut with a gun." Steve smiled. "I

should ask my wife if that's OK." Steve pulled out his cell phone. The set laughed.

Hunter pushed him playfully. "You can pistol whip me anytime." She meant it, too.

Perky asked, "Now, can we also play the game on our Xboxes and PS3s?"

Hunter blanked. She wasn't expecting that probing inquiry. She had no idea. So she did what she always did when she was stuck for a thought. She smiled and looked to her publicist, who was happy to answer the hard questions.

"Absolutely."

Hunter scooted forward to the edge of the couch. "The object of the game is to make your way from your penthouse apartment at the Sunset Marquis Hotel. When you leave, all you're wearing is panties and a bra. Boys are wearing their boxer briefs. You have at your disposal a platinum American Express card, the keys to your Porsche, or a money clip with a hundred thousand dollars, and a Magnum forty-four. You need to get to the Beverly Wilshire Hotel, where BMI is hosting the rap awards. There's a million-dollar-a-plate dinner followed by a silent auction."

Gretchen understood. She was already playing the game on her phone. "So the idea is to steal as much money as you can before you arrive at the party?"

"Exactly," said Hunter. "Of course you'll need shoes and a dress and accessories: jewelry, your doggy tote — you know, the necessities. Then you're going to want to bid on things at the auction. Like when you get to level nine, which is socialite level, you get to bid on staff for your summer home. If you win, you get a French tutor and an acting coach, and your kids will be famous."

All the sheep were playing the game on their phones. Hunter leaned over Weather Charlie's shoulder. Charlie was jabbing at his phone. "Why can't I rob this place? Their money is no good there?" The audience laughed.

"Well, you could rob them," Hunter said, oblivious to the joke. "But it's the welfare office. The most you could get is, like, two thousand dollars. And that's only if you kill the crack whore. I mean, just look at her. She's wearing a halter top."

"What's wrong with her halter top?" Weather Charlie volleyed.

Again the audience roared. Hunter noticed Kimberly's thumbs pumping away at her phone. "See, Kimberly has it. She followed the armored car to the private hospital."

"Wait, I get to shoot somebody in health care?" Charlie asked excitedly.

Steve Curtis put his phone down and told the audience about what they could look forward to in the next half-hour. More than half the audience had turned away from the monitors. They weren't interested in Hunter's five tips for better abs? They weren't interested in Serious Gretchen's report that 21 percent of America's children will go to bed hungry tonight? They didn't care about the pictures of Hunter's dog, Chi Chi, on safari in Africa?

Some of the people not interested in hard abs, hungry children, or animal irony were circling Country-Music Guy, all eyes fighting for a glimpse of the holy tortilla. As culture lay dying, Luke had been standing at the perimeter of the tortilla circle. He made his way back to me, and I couldn't believe what he reported.

Could this really be happening? The entire group was wrestling with an anxiety they couldn't comprehend. Nobody in the group had ever actually seen a real breast. TV breasts were always blurred. Some had seen a breast at birth, but the perspective-skewing proximity during breast-feeding combined with infantile amnesia led to a less-than-resolute image. Had they just taken a bite of Eden's fresh-baked apple pie? Why did something so pure make them feel so dirty? Was the answer in the tortilla?

"Get this," Luke said. "Bubba there says that when he hit the ground the corn patty actually spoke to him. He also says he can speak to it. Damn retard thinks he's the Tortilla Whisperer. If you shame them, he will come."

Some of the clowns were gathering near the tortilla, as were some of the reality hopefuls whose hopes had died.

Ice and Choi packed up the last of their gear. G shook my free hand.

"We want to tank ju for all jor help, *Escritor.* Ju and jor Chihuahua friend are to be commended. De strains we tagged here today may hold de key dat allows us finally to understand de unique animal dat lives in de hole."

"What about them?" I asked, pointing to the tortilla throng.

"Jess, I'm sorry to say dat we've seen dis before — de moral fervor. But wit dis new strain, de growth occurs at a much more alarming rate. It crosses all borders. Dis new 'Right' has become increasingly nationalistic. De great spirit of America is in danger of losing its wonderful identity. De lines between church and state are increasingly gray. Science is dere sworn enemy. Stem cells, abortion, birth control, gay marriage, *ay.* Dere focus is always out of focus."

"Like their tits," Luke joked.

"De world outside de hole is so rich in beauty," G continued. "It is just waiting to be discovered and explored. We need to teach de world dat de answer is in front of us, not up in some imagined heaven, not down on de ground. It's not a phone or an image. It is forward." G pointed to the horizon at the end of the sound stage, the horizon where the sun would have set. I thought of Zoë.

G saluted me. "Morgan Beale." Then Luke. "Chihuahua." Then, after a knowing pause: "Look forward. It is where de light will come from. De answer is forward."

Choi tossed him his goggles, and G climbed behind the wheel of the Jeep. Choi and Ice buckled up as the engine turned over. Choi snapped off a salute, as did Ice. G hit the gas. The Jeep sped down the ramp and disappeared into the hole.

They were gone.

RUN, BIG CHIMP, RUN!

The reality hopefuls had formed a procession to see the tortilla. Luke watched the hopefuls shuffle past the holy artifact.

"Why isn't there a procession for the man in the hole, the lost writer who started all of this?" Luke asked, turning from the lunacy. "You know what I think? It's because people can't identify with writers. They're not pretty enough. Writers don't sponsor exercise videos or fad diets. A writer would never seek out the cover of *People.* You know what would have changed things? If one of the chimps had fondled the writer before they threw him in the hole. *That* they understand. Why couldn't the chimps be terrorists? Or better yet, gays who are pro-abortion? Wait. Could they be illegal immigrants, too? Yeah, dirty homo baby killers! 'What can brown do for you?'"

The Eyewitness News music sang out. The monitors flickered alive with the familiar "Special News Report" banner. Full-frame was national anchor David Hume.

"Good day, America. I'm David Hume. Today, after an arraignment hearing for the Chimp Four, a daring escape by the suit-clad primates took place. Here is the exclusive video from our Eyewitness News Team."

The four chimps were being led out of the courthouse past a gauntlet of reporters, photographers, protesters, and supporters. Several police officers led the shackled primates through the circus. The Creative Artists chimp looked directly into the camera, espousing his innocence and telling his wife he'd be home soon. The male producer chimp looked like he was going to cry. His female partner tried to comfort him with shackled hands. Paramount Chimp looked defiant. He wore a look that said, *Nobody fucks with an Academy Award–winning producer.*

Then all hell broke loose. A tiny, effeminate male chimp skipped out of the crowd. He was wearing a perfectly tailored Brooks Brothers suit and was swinging a bottle of very expensive white wine. It was Marty Rudd, Paramount Chimp's former assistant and current lover. Marty Rudd created such a kerfuffle that Paramount Chimp was able to break free and slip behind the female cop escorting the female producer chimp. Paramount moved like a seasoned criminal as he seized the officer's gun and wrapped his arm around her neck. He pressed the barrel into her temple.

"Say hello to my leetle friend!"

Paramount Chimp waved his three accomplices behind him. They were all still shackled together. A veteran police officer boldly pointed his gun at Paramount, who growled, "Go ahead. Make my day!" He was the perfect executive, not an original thought in his head. If there had been a bakery nearby, he would have dropped the gun and reached for a cannoli.

The suits all backed up to a police car, and one by one they climbed inside. Creative Artists Chimp slid behind the wheel as Paramount Chimp barked the order to start the car. CAA Chimp knew what he was doing was wrong, but he did it anyway. After all, in the future he would have clients that Paramount Chimp could hire. There was also that screenplay that he'd been secretly writing for years. He would need a can-do chimp like Paramount on his side when it went out for coverage.

With the engine idling, Paramount Chimp ordered CAA Chimp to slide into the passenger seat. Paramount took the wheel and pulled the keys to the cuffs from the belt of his terrified captive. In a flash, he kicked the terrified policewoman to the ground and floored the gas. The car skidded wildly as it sped out of sight.

Across the sound stage, the back doors of the news van sprang open. A frantic Kevin Mackey rolled out and hit the ground, naked from the waist down. Totally naked Segment Producer Missy Wright hastily pulled her Eyewitness News jacket over her bare breasts as she pulled Kevbo's boxers up over her package.

"Yes, sir. I'm on it," she said into her phone. "We'll have Brock on camera right away."

Kevin Mackey couldn't find his shorts, so he grabbed the first thing that came to hand: Missy Wright's jeans. A surprisingly good fit. He shouldered the camera and ran for the hole.

Brock Robinson staggered through the doors of the flagship Starbucks, wiping a towel across his face to rub off the pumpkin lines. Missy Wright ran to him. Well, hobbled quickly. Her penis looked horribly cramped in the home of Kal-El, son of Jor-El. Kevin Mackey grabbed a power cable and made the male-to-female connection with ease.

On the monitor, a line of fifty other police vehicles was chasing the stolen cruiser across the freeway, a vehicular comet hurtling through space. The chimps weaved dangerously in and out of traffic. The Eyewitness News helicopter was right on top of them.

Brock Robinson took his mark next to the hole. Any second now, national anchor David Hume could call him to report. Brock would have to remind the TV viewers why these chimps were so dangerous.

Nobody was watching Hunter. She wasn't watching the police chase. Why should she? She didn't care about the writer in the hole. She didn't care about the chimps who put him in there. Hunter didn't care about anything. She didn't care about her entourage or the stunt man that liked to break the skin on her ass with his teeth. She stared down at her phone. Nothing. Anyone who might call was watching the chase. She texted someone. No return text. She dialed a number and pretended to be connected. Nobody was watching Hunter, and she couldn't stand it. Hunter didn't know how to be an afterthought. I always thought I wanted what Hunter had. I suddenly felt very sad for her.

The police chase had become a full-fledged ring in the media circus. Traffic congested. The Eyewitness News chopper still hovered over the action. The chimps were speeding along the shoulder, passing a steady stream of crawling cars. Time for action. The chimps on the run turned down an off ramp and onto surface streets.

Paramount navigated the stolen cop car through lights and pedestrian traffic. The Eyewitness News camera zoomed in on the defiant studio chimp shaking his gun at the world. Even the female producer chimp was getting into the act. Her middle finger told the world how she felt. The only creature with a larger penis than the female segment producer is the female feature-film producer. There is an adage in Hollywood, often stated but not scientifically substantiated: once you go female producer, you never go back.

The Eyewitness News camera retreated to a wide shot just as the stolen squad car approached a spike strip and roadblock.

Paramount Chimp had green-lighted more than thirty-five action films in the past three years. All of these films starred A-listers and had no discernible plot or structure. How could the police believe that a simple spike strip could stop a man who had disavowed any belief in the laws of physics? Didn't the police think Paramount Chimp might be able to levitate the car over the strip just by using his mind? The movies reflected real life, didn't they? Could law enforcement be this naive?

The stolen cruiser hit the spike strip and lost pressure in all but one tire — that tire being the spare in the trunk. How could this be? This doesn't happen in the movies. The *Good Day, America* team and the Actors of the Corn frowned in confusion. They needed an explanation. Should they look to the holy tortilla for an answer? If the rules that the movies have set forth could be compromised, what else had they been lying about to us? Models *can't* fly? Next thing you'll try to tell me is that my favorite rock star *isn't* a vampire. The nerve.

The wounded police cruiser shuddered to a stop. All four doors flew open at once, and the four chimps raced off in different directions. Six solid men in blue tackled the young male producer chimp. They pulled their nightsticks out and were beating the poor neophyte into submission.

Another ten in blue, guns drawn, had surrounded the female producer chimp. She was taunting the arresting posse. "You're nothings in this world! I've done the accounting on at least *ten* blockbusters, and I'm friends with some of the biggest eight-hundred-pound gorillas in town!" She singled out a young cop who had trained a taser on her. "My cock is most definitely bigger than yours! You're Irish. All cops are Irish. Don't you go to the movies? Micks have small dicks!"

The young cop lowered his aim and tased her enormous package. She crumbled as the boys in blue pounced.

CAA Chimp ran a few feet and stopped. He did what

every other agent in his position would have done. He raised his arms in defeat. If it wasn't going to be easy, he didn't want anything to do with it. His clients did all the running while he collected a commission. There would be no commission at the end of this race, so why bother?

Paramount Chimp was another story. Nobody was going to take him alive. He fled from the police cruiser, waving his stolen weapon. Bystanders leapt out of the way. He ran into oncoming traffic. With his gun in plain view, he stepped into the center lane and lowered the weapon to stop the next approaching vehicle. He wasn't moving. If the vehicle didn't stop, it would run him over. The Eyewitness News camera revealed the approaching doom.

Wait, we'd seen this type of truck before. Bright-red letters: FEMA. It was a FEMA relief crew. Paramount cocked the hammer, and the truck driver hit the brakes. Smoke poured out from the tire wells. The brakes were failing. Again. Was this Lloyd Keillor's truck? Or do all the vehicles at this top-notch government agency have faulty breaks?

A man leaned out of the driver's-side window and waved frantically at Paramount. It was the tallest of the *Good Day, America* grips, the one G had entrusted with the life of the man who deserved a second chance. Yes, this was indeed Lloyd Keillor's truck. The vehicle was slowing, but there wasn't enough real estate for the task at hand. Paramount casually stepped out of the way just as the truck rolled to a stop in the middle of the intersection.

He pointed his weapon into the cab and ordered the grip out of the truck. As the studio chimp slid behind the wheel, three other grips jumped out of the truck and ran for safety. Paramount put the truck in gear, and the chase resumed.

He drove through the mean streets of L.A. — Sunset Boulevard, Beverly Hills. In no time, he would be near the flagship Starbucks where all this began. The Eyewitness News chopper hovered above the truck like a wasp over an orchid. The cops paraded behind. People lined the street, cheering the passing FEMA truck.

The masses love the blockbusters that Paramount Chimp gives them every summer. They love movies based on rides from their favorite amusement parks. They love movies based on their favorite TV shows. They especially love movies based on movies they've never seen but have heard of. They love their movies to include the numbers 1, 2, 3, and 4. What? Paramount Chimp was bringing us a 5 this year? This one takes place in space? Run, big chimp, RUN!

Paramount ran red light after red light. Everyone on the streets of L.A. had pulled over to watch the chase on their phones. The entire country stood still.

Then I saw it. The FEMA truck was closing in on the flagship Starbucks. It crossed into the right lane and sped for the hole. Was that Paramount's destination? The hole? Smoke rose from the brakes. Too late. Big Chimp Paramount and the stolen truck disappeared into the void. The squad cars all screeched to a halt. Men in blue jumped from their cars and surrounded the hole, weapons drawn and trained into the dark. The Eyewitness News chopper hovered above the chasm.

As quickly as the truck had disappeared into the hole, it reappeared on the sound stage, skidding out of the dark and onto the lot in front of the Starbucks. Paramount fought to bring the wayward truck under control. It bounced wildly and sped past Brock, Kevin Mackey, and Missy Wright. Brock pointed at Kevin as he ran after the out-of-control truck. This would get him that anchor job!

Kevbo captured the image of skidding tires as Paramount screeched past the line of reality hopefuls and through the tortilla followers. People leapt out of the way as the government-issue truck bounced over the red carpet, past the monitors, past the ever-dwindling audience, and crashed through the doors of the flagship Starbucks, finally resting atop the couch on the *Good Day, America* set.

Smoke cleared as Paramount climbed from the wreckage, still carrying the stolen revolver. His free hand held a small canvas bag. Brock stood just outside the crash site. He was going to his microphone, but, before he could speak, Paramount crossed through the debris, held the bag aloft, and screamed at the top of his lungs, "I HAVE A BOMB!"

Brock dropped the microphone and ran out of the frame, screaming like a girl. Guess that anchor job would have to wait. The Actors of the Corn stampeded off the set. Steve Curtis also screamed like a girl. Gretchen and Kimberly tried to console him. Weather Charlie and Bob Botty ran through the broken glass to the safety around the hole.

All that remained on camera were Paramount and his bomb.

CITIZEN BOTTY

Where did Paramount get a bomb? On second thought, if anyone was capable of acquiring a bomb, it was Paramount. Everybody remembered his stint at MGM. It brought the studio to its knees. At MGM, any mention of the remake of *Casablanca* with that hot, leggy Latina pop star as Rick Blaine or the version of *Breakfast at Tiffany's* set on a futuristic space colony led to immediate dismissal. To say nothing of *On the Waterfront* as told through the eyes of a single mother of three who discovers her new union-busting boyfriend is a lesbian. Yes, Paramount was most definitely capable of producing a bomb. He said he had a bomb? He had a bomb. That was what the powers at big-time Network Central had decided. They abandoned their live broadcast from the hole until the situation was under control again.

Everyone on the sound stage evacuated into the hole. The tram that brought the reality hopefuls in now ferried Starbucks Nation to safety. Country-Music announced that he and his congregation would forgo the tram. The holy tortilla would lead them to the promised hole. He marched into the void, his ever-increasing congregation disappearing behind him. The clown photographers snapped away at Hunter and the other Actors of the Corn as they piled into the helicopter. Hunter waved and smiled. I felt nothing. For the first time that I could remember, Hunter meant nothing.

With no one to shoot or taunt, the clowns and their cameras shuffled into the dark. The *Good Day, America* team climbed into a limo bound for the safety of the hole. Steve Curtis hadn't stopped crying since the initial impact of the FEMA truck. Serious Gretchen and Perky Kimberly followed him and disappeared behind the limo's tinted glass. Weather Charlie took one last picture for a fan standing next to Bob Botty, then climbed into the limo.

Bob Botty remained behind. After all, he had been a decorated member of the LAPD bomb squad. When the sound stage and its inhabitants were safely inside the hole, Bob Botty would subdue Paramount and then defuse the bomb.

Brock Robinson was nowhere to be found. He had jumped screaming — like a girl — into the hole and would never return. He blew his chance at a network anchor chair, but there were dozens of entertainment magazine shows that would want his photogenic talents. He could bring his considerable reporting skills to the red carpet with hard-hitting questions like, "Who are you wearing this evening?" and "Who's your date?"

Kevin Mackey rolled down the sleeves of his shirt, dousing the flames on his forearms. He adjusted Missy Wright's jeans and reported on the evacuation to national anchor David Hume. He closed his taped segment as the last of the trams rolled into the hole. Missy Wright gave him a thumbs up and then adjusted her balls. Together they climbed into the Eyewitness News van and followed the *Good Day, America* trailer into the void.

Not a soul remained on the sound stage except for the big brooding chimp from Paramount, Bob Botty, and me. Luke was gone. Had he been swept up in the evacuation? Did one of the reality hopefuls scoop him up? Was he trapped in someone's doggy tote?

"Luke? *Luke!*"

Nothing.

Bob Botty's metallic body, covered with countless signatures from the rich and famous, rolled slowly toward the flagship Starbucks. He was in bomb-defuse mode, every movement slow and calculated. Big Chimp Paramount didn't look the least bit intimidated. He'd been dealing with robots his whole life. That's what people in the film business were — robots programmed to do as they were told. Paramount couldn't be bothered any longer. He set the canvas bag down and stepped through the broken doors of the flagship Starbucks. He circled around the lumbering robot, gave a quick French salute to the hole — "Fuck you, hole!" — and strolled into the darkness.

The robot loved by millions rolled through the debris and picked up the bag, slowly turning it over. Falling from the bag were two flares, a small medical kit, and a tiny orange roadside safety cone. The bag was just a FEMA emergency kit — standard issue for all government vehicles.

Bob Botty's robotic arm reached down for the flare. It did look like a stick of dynamite. When Bob Botty's other arm reached for the top of the flare, the plastic cap pulled free, and the flare ignited. Then Botty picked up the orange roadside cone. He rolled toward the wrecked FEMA truck and set the orange safety cone next to the driver's-side door. Then he laid the burning flare next to the wreck. Gas leaking from the truck ignited. The entire wreck went up in flames.

"ABORT! ABORT!" his robotic voice called.

Citizen Botty kicked it into high as he rolled from the fire. He zoomed across the lot, made his way down the ramp, and dropped into the void.

The flagship Starbucks caught fire. The flames were right on top of me, yet I felt no heat. Then I remembered: *I'm not here. I'm the writer. I'm not on camera.*

The FEMA truck, the set of *Good Day, America,* the television monitors, the red carpet, the audience barriers, the flagship Starbucks — everything burned to the ground.

ALONE IN THE HOLE

It didn't take long for the store to crumble into a pile of ash. Nothing was left. Just me, my desk, and the Starbucks drink dispenser. The ash cooled almost instantly.

Out of the hole came a man on a front-load tractor, followed by a beat-up, old blue pickup with a side placard that read "Arturo Kennedy's Gardening Service." The front loader lowered its enormous scoop and began to push the debris into the hole. It made a good twenty passes until the entire mess that was once the Whitehouse of Starbucks Nation was gone. The front loader then turned around and went back into the hole. The gardener from the beat-up truck pulled a leaf blower from the truck bed. He yanked the pull cord, blew the remaining dust into the hole, and then drove back into the void.

My arm was still stuck in the Starbucks drink dispenser in the middle of an otherwise immaculate sound stage. The stars twinkled above the HOLLYWOOD sign.

To the west, where the sun would set, I heard what sounded like a door opening. Blinding light poured into the sound stage. I used my free hand to shield my eyes, but as quickly as the light blazed it disappeared again. My eyes fought to readjust to the darkness.

A silhouette walked across the sound stage toward the hole. The figure was carrying a votive candle, the kind you find at a church or by the side of the road where someone had died. The figure stopped above the dark end of the hole and set the candle at the edge. The shape stood with head bowed, holding what looked like a rose in its hand. When the silhouette raised its head, my heart shattered.

It was Zoë.

She tried to smile as she wiped away a tear. Then she threw the rose into the hole. "This is so no one will forget the man in the hole. I will miss him. I loved you, Morgan. I really loved you."

I wanted to call out to her, but she wouldn't hear me. I was the writer. She turned away, made her way to the west, and stepped into the sun. The door closed and left me in darkness.

For the second time since I was eighteen years old, I cried. I cried for everyone in the hole. I cried for the parents whose children had died in the hole of war. I cried for the people who died in those buildings in New York in the name of God. I cried for children who are starving, for the broken people who are dying of AIDS and cancer. I cried for the people who lost their loved ones to accidents. I cried for every ounce of pain I'd inflicted on anyone in this world. I cried for all those caught up in the lie. I cried for Zoë. I cried for me. I cried.

Then I heard a voice above me, a familiar voice. Luke was smiling down from the chair at the end of the director's crane. Chihuahua no more, Luke the madman was back.

He swooped down. "CUT! AND PRINT IT! Crackerjack, Morgan, crackerjack! Burning down the Starbucks? Everything into the hole? No thumb holding you down, that's for sure. Fuck the man! Into the hole! Technology? Into the hole! The whole goddamn machine belongs in the hole. And the thing with Zoë? The only thing that doesn't come out of or end up in the hole is the only thing you ever wanted. Love escapes the hole. Crackerjack, FUCKING CRACKERJACK!"

My desperation was mounting. I wanted to ask him a question, but I was afraid of the answer. Still, it needed to be asked. "Am I dead?"

Luke's smile withered. "Yes. Out there, behind that door . . . your heart has stopped."

Luke climbed off the crane, standing face-to-face with me. He reached into his pocket and fished out a fistful of change. He plugged it into the Starbucks dispenser until the light blinked "Make Your Selection." He pressed an illuminated button. The clamp holding my wrist released. I pulled my left arm from the machine. I was free.

Luke walked toward the western horizon. “Come on.”

He opened the door where the sun would set, and I stepped into the light.

MORGAN BEALE R.I.P.

I have fallen only inches from the phone company's hole. My left hand lies next to what is left of the Starbucks antidote. A young paramedic tears open my shirt and places the defibrillator paddles on my chest. My body leaps from the shock.

Nothing.

Again I am prepped, paddled, and zapped.

Nothing. The photographers who followed me snap pictures of my lifeless body. A young girl records every sordid detail on her video phone. The Starbucks baristas stare, motionless. I feel Luke's hand on my shoulder.

"Morgan . . ."

I turn to the familiar voice.

"Go home."

What? What is he saying? Where's home?

"It's not time for you. Go home. Go to Zoë. . . . She's alone now. She can save you."

"I don't . . ."

"Some people's hearts have to stop before they can start again." He looks down at my lifeless body. "We had a laugh, didn't we? — down there."

"Yeah . . ."

"Yeah, we did. I'll see ya 'round." He turns away, chuckling to himself. "FEMA in the hole. Clowns into a wall. Elves with rifles. God, that's funny!" He turns back. "You always were the funny one."

He takes no more than a few steps, and then just vanishes.

Prepped, paddled, and zapped.

They say I was dead a full three minutes before they found a heartbeat.

I am alive. I am home.

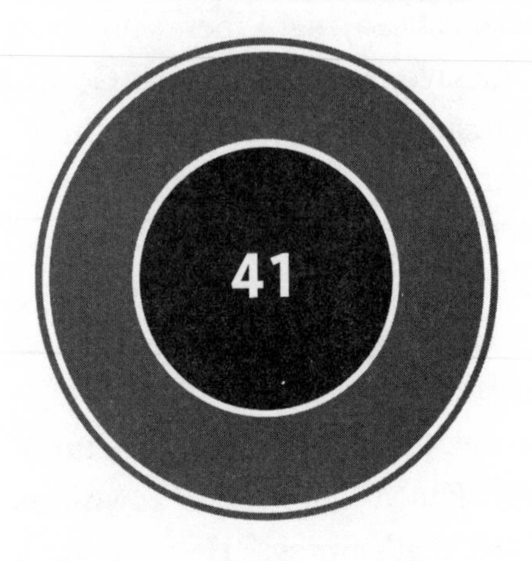

LIVING THE EPILOGUE OF MY LIFE

Today is exactly one year to the day since I died. I have marked the occasion by taking an apartment in the South of France. Every morning I take my single espresso in a café that overlooks a country market. Every morning I eat a croissant with apricot jam.

The pace is slow here. People walk here. I walk here. I like watching the men at their chessboards. I like listening to them talk. I like watching the young girls giggle about their boyfriends. I like the old woman who chases her chickens out of her vegetable garden. I like the old man in the bakery who laughs at everything. He has taught me to laugh again. I like the couple who owns the wine shop. They have taught me to enjoy my life. I like watching Zoë read. She looks up from her book and catches me watching her.

"What?" she says.

I smile that smile I'd forgotten. "Nothing." I think how much I love her.

She glances at the pen and notebook she bought for me. "Are you stuck?"

"No."

"What are you writing about?"

"About how you saved me."

She grins playfully. Under the table her foot rests against my leg. The weight of her body against mine makes me feel safe. She turns back to her book. I turn to mine. I begin to write.

It was the dishwasher at the hotel bar who taught me the secret handshake.